ANGEL'S HEART

CHARLENE TESS
JUDI THOMPSON

Copyright © September 1, 2023
by Charlene Tess and Judi Thompson
All rights reserved.

No part of this publication may be reproduced, distributed, or transmitted in any form or by any means, including photocopying, recording, or other electronic or mechanical methods, without the prior written permission of the publisher, except as permitted by U.S. copyright law. For permission requests, contact novelsbyTessThompson@gmail.com.

The story, all names, characters, and incidents portrayed in this production are fictitious. No identification with actual persons (living or deceased), places, buildings, and products is intended or should be inferred.

Acclaim for Secondhand Hearts Series

Accidental Angel (Book 1)

"OMG, this was an Amazing book. I started it in one day and read til the end at 3am. I couldn't put the book down. I loved every second of it. A must read"

"This was a good story about two people finding themselves and finding a chance at love. Well written. Good job!"

Angel's Heart (Book 2)

"Do yourself a favor and read Take a break from all the ugliness and hatred in the world and bathe yourself in a story of love and kindness. Even in difficult times, these people retain their love and dignity."—Charles Bourland produced screenwriter and author

"Angel's Heart was a delight from start to finish. With only a couple of exceptions, these are people we'd all want in our lives. Great characters. – Great story. "

CHAPTER 1

A hard-driving rain pelted the car's windshield, splattering on the glass faster than the wiper blades could erase it. An unusual weather pattern flooded the streets of Southern California with record rainfall.

James Ross turned his head and spoke to his son Matt, who sat in the backseat. His arms were folded around his skinny body. "How ya doing, buddy? Your stomach still hurting?"

"A little bit, but I still don't feel so good. I feel like I could puke."

James chuckled and said, "You've got your barf bag, right?"

"Yeah, Dad," he whined indignantly.

Matt had missed school the last two days while suffering from a stomach bug, and he wasn't improving. James would call tomorrow and take him to see a doctor. The kid was never sick, but his appetite had been off for the last few weeks, and he hadn't been himself.

A bright flash of lightning off to the right, followed by a crash of thunder, startled them both as James gripped the steering wheel tighter, and Matt squealed. "We're almost home, kiddo."

Water pooled on the sides of the street near the curb, and James slammed on the brakes, causing the car to fishtail on the wet asphalt, when something ran in front of his car, and he heard a sickening thump.

James's hands were shaking when the car screeched to a complete stop,. He knew he had hit something. Good Lord, please don't let it be a person. He jumped out of the car while calling over his shoulder, "Stay there, Matt. Stay in the car."

The rain still fell in buckets, and wiping his eyes, he spotted an animal lying on the road. A dog. He gently touched it to see if it was alive and was relieved to hear a soft whine.

"Dad, Dad, what is it?"

He looked up to see his son, dripping wet, standing there in the rain. "I told you to wait in the car. You're already sick. Do you want to get pneumonia?"

"But it's a dog. Is he going to die? Please don't let him die." Matt was sobbing and reached down to touch the dog's wet fur. "Please don't let him die."

Matt had always been a sensitive child who felt things more deeply than most of his friends, and those emotions intensified after the death of his mother five years earlier.

"Hurry, Matt. Get the blanket I keep in the back. We'll bundle him up and take him to the vet. I'm sure there's an emergency clinic around here somewhere."

~

DOCTOR ANGELA MICHAELS pushed her glasses up on her forehead and looked at the notes she'd written concerning the last patient she'd seen. A miniature poodle, Missy, with sudden onset of vomiting and diarrhea. The blood work had ruled out any significant issues, such as diabetes or kidney disease, and Angela had placed her on IV fluids.

The owners would pick up the little dog in the morning, and she would advise them to follow up with their regular vet for further testing. Emergency services for dogs were expensive, just like they were for people, and she tried to be as easy on their pocketbooks as possible.

When the receptionist in the small lobby called out to her, Angela quickly closed her computer, slipped on her glasses, and hurried toward the door. A soaking-wet man met her, carrying a dog covered by a blanket. A small boy followed closely on his heels.

"I hit this dog with my car. I'm so sorry. It was raining hard, and I didn't see him until he was right in front of me."

Angela's voice was calm and reassuring as she said, "I'm Doctor Michaels. Let's take him into the exam room, and I'll take a look. Place him on the table and then take a seat in the waiting room. I'll come and talk to you as soon as possible. I'll have the receptionist bring you some towels."

She took in the stricken face of the boy and reached out to touch his shoulder. "I'll take excellent care of your dog."

"He's not my dog. He …" Tears pooled in his big brown eyes, and his lips quivered.

"He doesn't belong to us," James said. "He just ran out in front of my car. My son's obviously very upset, and so am I."

His attitude impressed Angela. Sadly, too many people wouldn't have bothered to bring a stray dog to an emergency clinic for care. She hoped she didn't have to give the boy sad news.

After leaving the small room, Angela turned to her assistant and removed the blanket from the dog. She checked its eyes and gums, gently felt its body, and gave instructions for treatment to her assistant.

LATER, when she walked into the lobby, the man and his son stood immediately, and Angela took a seat across from them and motioned for them to sit back down.

"I'm sorry I didn't introduce myself or my son earlier. I'm James Ross, and this is my son, Matt." The eyes that met hers were a vivid green, and she stared into them longer than she intended. His hair had dried, and she noticed his soft smile and handsome face.

She blinked and looked away as she said, "The first thing to know is that he is a she. I've examined the injuries, done blood work, and placed her on fluids. Fortunately, she doesn't appear to have any internal injuries, but she has a fractured leg requiring surgery. That's the good news."

"What's the bad news?" the boy said, leaning forward. His hair was dry now and curled into a million soft, dark brown swirls.

"Even though you're not the owner, you are responsible for her care because you brought the dog into the clinic. I can donate my time but not the medications. She didn't have a collar or tags and wasn't chipped, so I will have to classify her as a stray. She's young. I would say around five or six months and probably a border collie and shepherd mix."

"I don't care about the money. Do the surgery if that's what she needs."

"And what about after the surgery? I can try to find a rescue group that will foster her, but that's not a guarantee."

James glanced at his son's troubled face and then back at Angela. "We'll be taking her home. When will you do the surgery?"

She looked at her watch and said, "I'll do it now, and if all goes well, you can pick her up tomorrow afternoon."

JAMES RAKED his fingers through his messy hair and felt shocked at what he'd agreed to so quickly. He would have gladly given his son anything he wanted within reason, and Matt had always wanted a dog. James was a professional baseball player who traveled eight months out of the year for several days at a time, while Matt stayed with his grandparents. A dog hadn't been a possibility.

But since he was retiring at the end of this season, which wasn't that far away, he could spend all his time at home with Matt and the dog. He would make it work for Matt's sake.

Doctor Michaels returned to the waiting room with a clipboard and explained the permission and financial responsibility documents that James needed to sign.

When he handed the papers to her, she removed her glasses and rubbed her eyes. He thought they were a lovely shade of golden brown fringed by long black lashes, and she wore her dark brown hair pulled back in a loose ponytail.

Something about her looked familiar, but he was sure he would have remembered if they had met before. She was a captivating beauty who seemed genuinely friendly and caring. Although he felt an instant spark of attraction, he didn't plan to do anything about it. He had too many responsibilities to think about dating. Besides, he'd probably never see her again after he picked up the dog tomorrow.

CHAPTER 2

Angela rubbed the back of her neck as she went to check on her most recent patient before she left for the night. She'd worked overtime on her shift, and her body felt every hour. Once they had cleaned up the dog, it was apparent she was a pretty thing with her black and white face and fluffy dark coat.

She thought about the man and his son and how happy the boy was when he learned they would take the dog home. She remembered the boy's name was Matt. A memory flashed in her mind, and she held it for a moment before quickly putting it away as her phone buzzed in her pocket.

When she saw Greg's name, she sighed and answered. "Hi, Greg. I'm sorry I didn't call, but things got crazy here."

"When I didn't hear from you, I got worried. You know it's raining cats and dogs outside." She heard him chuckle as if that was the funniest joke she'd ever heard.

She gave an obligatory laugh. "Ha, very funny. I'm fine. I had an emergency and worked overtime."

"They're going to pay you for that, right?"

"Of course, they're going to pay me. It's in my contract."

Greg was a lawyer and thought like one. They'd met six months earlier at a fundraiser his law firm supported for animal rights, and he had asked her out. Since then, they'd dated as often as two professionals with busy schedules could arrange.

For the past month, Greg had been pressuring her to move in with him. He had a lovely, spacious home and often commented on her tiny cracker box house and middle-class neighborhood. She liked Greg, but she also enjoyed her home and her neighbors, and she wasn't ready for the next step in their relationship.

"I'm getting ready to walk out the door. Let's talk tomorrow. Okay?"

"How about lunch? At that Italian place you like."

"Sorry, can't. I need to be back here at noon."

"You're not making this easy for us, Angela. You work constantly and never have time for me."

"That's not fair. I'm trying to pay off my school loans, so I can open my own practice. You knew that when we met."

"Then move in with me and save on rent. At least that way we'd see each other."

"I really don't want to talk about this right now. I'm at work."

"How about we meet for a late breakfast at that place across from your clinic? Around ten?"

She thought for a moment and finally said, "You're very persuasive."

"I can be when I want something, and I definitely want you."

After agreeing to breakfast, she ended the call and placed the phone back in her pocket. She took the time to check on each animal in its kennel and give an update and instructions to the next shift before walking out the back door.

The rain had made the air chilly, but instead of thinking

of her nice warm bed as she dodged puddles, she visualized a handsome face with deep-set green eyes and an arresting smile. A man with a son and probably a pretty wife.

∼

AFTER BREAKFAST, Angela felt wired from drinking too much coffee and having too little sleep. Thankfully, today Greg didn't push about her moving in but made it clear he planned to bring it up again soon.

The conversation mostly revolved around Greg, which was okay with Angela. She'd never been comfortable talking about herself. Too many ghosts in her closet.

The morning fog had given way to bright sunlight, and the sky was a cobalt blue with patchy white clouds. The air smelled clean and fresh, and the only reminder of yesterday's storm was the water pooling in the parking lot's low places.

Angela pressed the code to enter the clinic's back door and felt like she'd just left. She could have used a couple more hours of sleep but had agreed to breakfast because she felt guilty about having so little time to spend with Greg this week. Hoping she didn't look as tired as she felt, she smoothed down her hair.

"Good morning, Doctor Michaels," the vet assistant said as he closed a kennel door.

"Good morning, Tony. Anything come up that needs my attention? No complications, I hope."

"No, Patches is doing great."

"Patches?"

He pointed at the dog she had treated the night before. "Look at her markings. She looks like she has patches of black and white. I needed to call her something."

Angela opened the cage door, and a wagging tail and cold nose greeted her. "Well, look at you, feeling all better." She reached in, scratched behind the dog's ears, and was rewarded with a sloppy kiss.

"Have you taken her out yet?"

"Got the leash in my hand, ready to go. She ate a good breakfast."

Angela watched Tony gently lift the dog from the cage and lead it to the door. She looked at her watch, and because she was still a few minutes early, took the time to log into her computer and look up the contact information on Patches' adoptive family.

She picked up the phone and entered the number. After two rings, a deep voice answered.

"Hello, Mr. Ross. This is Doctor Michaels from the Twenty-four-hour Emergency Animal Clinic."

"Oh, yes. Did something happen? Matt will be devastated," he said, lowering his voice.

"Everything is fine. The surgery went well, and she's ready for you to pick her up. Do you want us to administer her basic vaccinations? She'll need them if you ever plan to board her."

"Oh sure, whatever the dog needs. Matt's jumping up and down for me to take him to the store to buy pet food and toys."

"I would also recommend you get a kennel. She will need to be kept quiet until her leg heals. When you pick her up, we will give you all the instructions to care for her wound."

"Can't thank you enough. We'll be there soon."

Angela hung up with a smile and looked at the list of scheduled patients waiting in the exam rooms. It was time to get to work.

She had almost finished suturing a deep cut on a sedated Labrador who had a chunk taken out of his side by an aggressive dog at a park when the receptionist entered the room.

"Dr. Michaels, there's this good-looking dude asking for you. You said to let you know when he got here," Rachel said.

"I don't recall telling you to be on the lookout for a good-looking dude."

"Well, no, that's me saying the good-looking part. You do know who he is, don't you?"

"Yes, James Ross and his son Matt is probably with him."

"Yeah, THE James Ross. The pitcher for San Diego."

Angela looked up with a confused expression. "So?"

"He's frigging famous. You never heard of him?"

She shook her head and said, "Sorry, no. I don't follow baseball. Would you tell him I'll be right out after I finish here?"

"That will be my pleasure."

"And, Rachel, go easy on him. He's entitled to privacy like everyone else, whether he's famous or not."

CHAPTER 3

*J*ames's eyes searched the clinic as he followed the young vet tech into the small exam room. He wasn't sure why he felt the need to make a better impression today than the one he'd made the night before when he had looked like a drowned rat. Today, he'd dressed casually in a blue chambray shirt and jeans, and his hair was neatly combed.

He sat down in one of the plastic chairs, looked around the small room, and noticed an antiseptic odor. A waist-high stainless-steel table sat in the middle of the room with a desk along one wall and three framed landscape prints on another. They helped make the windowless room feel less claustrophobic.

The door opened, and Doctor Angela Michaels entered. She led the fluffy black and white dog, who hopped on three legs while holding her injured hind leg off the floor. The doctor slipped the leash into James's hand, her hand brushing across his calloused fingers. The dog sat obediently, and James looked down into the big brown puppy dog eyes.

If dogs could smile, he'd swear that's what this one was doing.

"The staff has fallen in love with Patches," the doctor said.

James scrunched his forehead and raised one eyebrow higher than the other in confusion. "I'm sorry, who is Patches?"

A wide smile spread across Doctor Michaels' face. She was a pretty woman, but he thought she was downright beautiful when she smiled like that.

"I asked the same question this morning. One of the vet techs named her Patches. Most of our patients come to us with names. She's a smart dog and very well-behaved. It's hard to believe someone just let her wander alone outside on a rainy night."

James nodded and scratched Patches under the chin. The dog had not taken her eyes off him since entering the room and was panting contentedly.

Angela looked around the room and towards the door. "Where's Matt?"

"He wanted to come, but his stomach started hurting again, and he was running a fever. He's been fighting off a virus all week. My next stop after getting Patches home today is to take Matt to the pediatrician. I will let Matt name the dog, but Patches seems to fit, doesn't it?"

"Yes, it kinda does. I'm so sorry about Matt. Please tell him I hope he gets better soon because his new dog will need lots of attention." She gave him two printed sheets with instructions for caring for the injured leg and a recommendation to follow up with a local veterinarian to test for heartworms and other parasites. "If you'd like a list of veterinarians in the area, our receptionist will get that for you."

"Thanks, I'd appreciate that." He scanned the information and shook his head. "I think I'll stay home the next time there's a big rainstorm," he said, smiling as he folded and tucked the papers into his shirt pocket.

"Are you going to try to find the owner?"

"I'll look around for flyers to see if anyone lost her. Patches was on my street when she ran out in front of me, but I don't expect anyone will be looking for her."

Angela held out her hand and said, "You're a good man, Mr. Ross. It was nice meeting you and your son."

He took her small, delicate hand and shook it gently. "You're not too shabby yourself, Doctor Michaels." She rewarded him with another megawatt smile as he gently tugged on the dog's leash and turned to leave the room.

∽

JAMES PULLED his SUV into the three-car garage beside his old Dodge pickup. When he and Cindy were younger, before they had Matt, they'd splurged on a fancy sports car for him and a luxury car for her. But he'd held onto his truck, symbolizing his struggling college days and ball-playing days in the minors.

James was almost forty years old. Although he had enjoyed a distinguished career, and it would be hard to imagine life without baseball, he knew it was time to retire. He wanted to participate in his son's life while the boy was still young. Matt had turned twelve last spring, and he would be a teenager next year.

After Cindy died, he had to leave Matt in the care of his parents, or if necessary, his in-laws when he was on the road, which wasn't fair to them. It was his only choice at the time, but although they'd never complained, he knew they had already raised their families. It was time for them to travel and enjoy their retirement.

The house was quiet when he entered the kitchen from

the garage and found his mother standing in front of the stove. She turned and looked down in surprise. Her voice lilted in a sing-song cadence, "Oh, look what you have. What a precious little girl!" She dropped to her knees and let the dog lick her face.

She reached out a hand, and James helped her to her feet. "I hate to mention the obvious, but what will you do with her when you're out of town? I'm afraid my cats would stroke out if they had to suffer the company of a dog."

He opened his mouth to say Cindy's parents would keep her but immediately closed it when he remembered their white carpets and pristine household. Delegating a dog to the backyard all day wasn't a good option either. "I don't know yet. I'll think of something."

"You're a sucker, Jimmy Ross."

His mother was one of the few people that called him Jimmy. When he'd met Cindy, she'd teased him about the nickname and insisted he should be called James. She said Jimmy was a kid's name. How could he expect people to take him seriously? He'd been James ever since, except to his family.

"Matt looked at me with those big brown eyes, and he hasn't been feeling well. How could I tell him no? The kid doesn't ask for much. Maybe someone will advertise that they lost the dog, which will solve the problem."

James looked up to see Matt standing in the doorway with a stricken expression on his face. "No, Dad, no. You said she was mine." Matt dashed to the dog and threw his arms around her fluffy neck.

"Let's take her out back and let her do her business, and then we need to get her settled down in the crate and get the weight off that leg." James pulled his son close to him and held the leash with the other arm as they moved slowly toward the backyard.

ANGEL'S HEART

"I told you we could keep her, but someone might be missing her. She could belong to some other little boy."

"But he didn't take care of her, so he doesn't deserve to have her."

"We don't know the circumstances, so it's best not to judge. We'll have to wait and see if anyone is looking for her." He tousled his son's curly hair. "Are you feeling better?"

"Yes, a little. Do I still have to go to the doctor?"

"Yep." He unclipped the leash, and the dog moved gingerly through the grass, looking back toward them with each halting step as if checking to see if they were still there. "Have you thought of a name for your dog yet?"

"No, and I've been thinking."

"The nice people at the emergency clinic called her Patches. How does that sound?"

"She does have black and white everywhere. Is that what the pretty doctor named her?"

"Doctor Michaels said that one of the vet assistants named her, so that's what the doctor called her, too."

"Patches. Yeah, I like that. Let's call her Patches."

∼

THE PEDIATRICIAN'S office was painted a bright yellow, and they had decorated one wall with a mural of a blue ocean and children and animals playing in the surf. In one corner was a section with small tables and chairs where Matt had played when he was much younger.

Matt had been Doctor Brewer's patient since the boy was a newborn, and James and Cindy had always had great confidence and respect for the man. The doctor examined Matt closely and felt his abdomen, legs, and ankles. Then he looked into his mouth, ears, and eyes.

"Okay," the doctor said, "you can sit up now. Looks like a

virus, but to be sure, I'd like to do some bloodwork." He patted Matt on the knee and said, "Is that okay with you, Matt?"

Matt chewed on his lip, flashed a look at his dad, and then back at the doctor. "Will it hurt?"

"A little sting. That's all. You've probably felt worse falling off your bike."

Matt smiled bravely, and James stood beside him while the nurse drew the blood. To James's surprise, Matt kept his eyes on the needle while observing the entire process.

"That's so cool," Matt said, "and it didn't hurt at all."

"I'll call you with the results tomorrow. In the meantime, I've written a prescription for nausea. If he feels like it, there's no reason he can't go to school," the doctor said.

"Should I be concerned?" James asked.

"Let's wait until I get the blood tests back. We'll talk tomorrow."

A cloud of anxiety engulfed James as they walked out of the office. He had the impression that the doctor suspected something was seriously wrong with his son, and all James could do was wait for the other shoe to drop.

CHAPTER 4

Angela Michaels heard a cacophony of yipping and barking dogs as she opened the side door and stepped into Hollywood's Kennel. A woman dressed in jeans and a denim shirt looked up and waved. "Good morning, Doctor Michaels."

"Good morning, Marsha. Hollywood called and asked me to check on one of her guests."

Marsha laughed and said, "Not exactly one of our guests, more like a rescue. You know the boss is always taking in the strays, hoping to find them homes. She's in the back and can give you all the details."

Hollywood Madden had owned the dog kennel that bore her name for many years. It sat in a prime location between San Diego and Laguna Beach, California, and people from the local area and beyond trusted her to keep their beloved pets safe. Angela had known the lovely, yet somewhat eccentric older woman, for most of her life. Hollywood was one of a kind. All eyes followed her when she entered a room.

While Angela was a teenager trying to escape an unhappy

home, Hollywood had let her help feed and care for the boarded dogs. Later, while Angela attended the local college, Hollywood recommended Angela for a job with a local veterinarian. It was just what she needed to help her pay her tuition as she worked her way through school.

Angela could see Hollywood through the glass in the doorway leading to the back area of the kennel. The stout older woman usually had a turquoise necklace of one variety or another dangling in the hollow between her ample breasts. Today, it was a large stone set in silver, and she wore a loose and flowing multicolored peasant blouse. She had pulled her mane of alabaster hair back with a turquoise headband that accented her dark-lashed, robin's-egg-blue eyes.

Angela pushed open the door, thinking that finding another James Ross when you needed one would be nice, and suddenly there he was right in front of her. She stopped in her tracks and took in the scene before her. Hollywood was hosing down the biggest dog she'd ever seen, and James Ross held the dog's shoulders to keep him in place.

They both looked up simultaneously, and Angela was the first to speak. "Mr. Ross, what are you doing here? And what has Hollywood talked you into?"

"I didn't talk him into anything, missy," Hollywood said. "Jimmy and I go way back to when he and my son Shane were in school together."

"Hi, Doc," James said, giving her a friendly smile. "I realized I need a kennel to board Patches in when I'm out of town, and then I remembered this place. I hadn't thought about it in years."

Hollywood huffed and said, "Thanks a lot, kiddo. I haven't thought about you in ages either."

"You know I didn't mean it that way," he said, giving her a sheepish smile.

Hollywood brightened at his apology and turned to look at Angela. "My assistant had an emergency this morning, and everyone is busy with morning chores. I had to get Buster here ready for pickup. Normally, I could do it alone, but as you can see, he's a big fellow. Jimmy graciously agreed to help me." She wiped the soap from her brow with the back of her hand. "How do you two know each other?"

"Mr. Ross brought his dog to the emergency clinic the other night. We don't really know each other."

"Please call me Jimmy. It's less confusing that way. Why are you here?" he asked.

"And you can call me Angela. I'm the vet on call for the animals boarded here."

"She and I go way back too, but not as far back as you," Hollywood said.

"Small world," he said.

"Yes, it certainly is." Hollywood looked at James and then back at Angela and winked at her.

What was all that about? Angela thought. She shook her head and said, "You wanted me to look at one of the dogs. Marsha said something about a stray."

"Yeah, cute little thing looks like a mixture of dachshund and Chihuahua. I've found him a home, but I want to ensure he's healthy and ready to go. Can you do that for me, sweetie?"

"Of course. Where is he?"

"In one of the holding cages in the back. I'll join you after I finish with the big boy here."

Angela smiled and wondered to which big boy she was referring. She couldn't help noticing that the human one was awesome looking, with his dark hair falling into his eyes and spots of water splashed on his shirt that stretched across his broad chest.

JAMES COULDN'T HELP STARING at the woman standing in front of him. Doctor Angela Michaels wasn't wearing her long white lab coat today, and he could see that she had a curvaceous figure and filled out the blouse tucked into her skinny jeans very well. Her dark hair hung loose to her shoulders, and he could see the straps of a small backpack.

Something about her pulled at him, and although he had tried not to think about her, his mind had drifted to her a lot over the last few days.

"Hey, did you hear what I said?" Hollywood poked him on the shoulder.

"No, sorry."

"I asked if you needed me to wipe the drool off your face?"

He frowned. Was the woman a mind reader? He watched Angela walk through the large door toward the kennels, where he'd said goodbye to Patches a short time earlier.

He didn't feel too bad about leaving the sweet dog. She had an indoor-outdoor space, and they would exercise her and let her play with other dogs several times a day. After dropping Matt off at school, he had brought Patches here. He was due at the stadium at noon for the bus ride to the airport.

"I don't know what you're talking about. The doctor was nice and kind to my son and me."

"Yeah, Shane told me about losing your wife and that you had a young son. I'm so sorry for your loss, Jimmy. That must be hard."

"I'm sorry for yours, too. Mr. Madden was a great guy, and I had some good times with your whole family as a kid. It's a shame that Shane and I drifted apart. He went away to medical school, and I went to the minors. Maybe we can reconnect when I retire, and I'm back here full time."

"He married a lovely woman. She's a pediatric nurse, and he and another doctor have opened a clinic in the city. I know he would love to get together with you."

Hollywood handed James a large towel and said, "Better step back, or he'll shake water all over you. Why don't you go back and say goodbye to Patches and Angela, too?"

"Please tell Shane hello for me."

"I certainly will."

James found Angela examining a tiny little dog, the polar opposite of the dog he'd been holding for Hollywood. He watched her pick it up and croon high-pitched doggie words to him before replacing him in the kennel.

"I came to say goodbye and thank you again for the other night."

"You don't have to do that. It was my job, and I'm glad Patches found a good home."

"Where are you off to now? Back to work at the emergency clinic?"

She looked down at her watch and said, "No, not for a few more hours. I'm glad I saw you. I wanted to suggest that you bring Patches back in so I can check her leg since you don't have a regular vet. Because I did the surgery, there will be no charge."

"I'll be out of town for five days. Will that be too long?"

She shook her head and said, "No, that's about right." She pulled a card out of her backpack and said, "When you're back in town, call to find out what days I'm working."

She picked up her backpack, and he said in a rush, "Have coffee with me?"

"Now?"

"You said you don't have to be at work for a couple of

hours." He was holding his breath, wanting her to say yes. He quickly added, "As a thank you. It meant a lot to Matt. He's a sensitive kid, and you made him feel special."

She hesitated a moment and finally said, "All right. Sure, I'll have coffee with you."

CHAPTER 5

Angela ordered a regular coffee with cream and one sugar and noticed that James had taken a bottle of water out of the cooler. When they slid into a booth and sat across from each other, she said, "You're not a coffee guy?"

He twisted the lid off the plastic bottle and set it on the table. "No, never got the hang of it, and as a professional athlete, I didn't want all that caffeine. I try to eat healthy …."

"And it shows." Her face flushed crimson, and she couldn't believe she'd said that out loud. "I'm sorry. I didn't mean to imply." She rushed on. "Well, actually, I did mean. Oh, never mind. Just shoot me now and put me out of my misery."

He gave her a lopsided grin and said, "How do you know Hollywood?"

"I met her through an after-school volunteer program as a kid, and I spent many of my Saturdays and Sundays playing with the dogs." He tipped the bottle and took a long drink of the cold water.

She wound her finger around a lock of her long dark hair and then fiddled with the plastic lid on her cup. She was nervous sitting across from this handsome man while fighting her attraction to him. For all she knew, he could be married. Besides, she was involved with Greg, although she realized her heart never thumped like this when she was with him.

"So, you're a professional ballplayer?"

"Yeah, but how did you know I play baseball?"

"The receptionist at the emergency clinic recognized you. Are you famous?"

"That should be a blow to my ego if you have to ask," he laughed, "but I'm only well-known in the baseball world. In the scheme of things, I'm small potatoes."

"At least you are potatoes," she laughed.

"I'm retiring at the end of the season, which is less than a month from now. Unless we make the playoffs, which doesn't seem likely."

"You're so young to retire."

"Tell that to my body. No, it's time. I want to be with Matt every day and reconnect with old friends."

"Did you grow up with Hollywood's kids? I've met a few."

"Yeah, there's five of them, all with movie character names. You do know that her real name is Delores, don't you? Her late husband dubbed her Hollywood because they met and fell in love at the movie theater where she worked. She was crazy for all things involving films and movie stars."

"Now that's a romantic tale." She held the coffee with both hands, and it felt warm. The way Jimmy looked at her warmed her even more, and she hoped she wouldn't blush. Quickly changing the subject from romance and love, she said, "How is Matt doing? You said he was sick again, and you were taking him to the doctor."

"He's better. They ran some bloodwork. It didn't reveal any infection, and his blood count was good. He's back in school and sports."

ANGEL'S HEART

"Does he play baseball like you?" She sipped her coffee and noticed he'd downed most of his bottle of water.

"He does in the spring and summer, but I've had to miss most of his games. Thankfully, my mom and dad video all of them for me, so I can watch them later."

He must have seen the unspoken question on her face because he said, "My wife, Cindy, passed away several years ago. When I'm out of town with the team, my parents, or occasionally Cindy's parents, take care of Matt, but he has a closer relationship with mine."

He raked his fingers through his hair, finished off his water, and replaced the cap on the empty bottle. "She was a great mother, even though she had a busy law practice. We met in college and married after she finished law school."

"I'm so very sorry for your loss and for Matt's. I assumed you were divorced since you never mentioned a wife."

His eyes met hers, and she could see the pain reflected in them. "She died from an aortic aneurysm that was completely unexpected and instantaneous."

"I can't imagine how hard that's been for you while raising Matt and continuing your career." She reached out and touched his hand, and he didn't pull away.

∼

WHAT WAS WRONG WITH HIM? He never talked about himself, and especially not about Cindy. His entire purpose for asking Angela out for coffee was to get to know her better, and he'd learned exactly zip. He only learned that she had met Hollywood when she was young, but he already knew that because of an earlier conversation with Hollywood.

He looked down at her small soft hand with short, trimmed nails polished a shade of pale pink. She didn't wear jewelry except for a small silver pendant on a short chain. He wanted to know all about her life, but she beat him to the punch before he could ask.

"You said to call you Jimmy, but you introduced yourself as James. Hollywood calls you Jimmy. James is a sort of buttoned-up name. You know, for a suit and tie kind of guy. You seem more laid back, like a Jimmy to me. After all, you got soaking wet in the cold rain to rescue a hurt dog. Which name do you like better?"

"I was called Jimmy all my life until I went to college. All my old friends and relatives still call me that."

"Then, with your permission, that's what I'll call you too." She looked at her watch and said, "Oh gee, I've got to run. Thanks for the coffee and the conversation. I'll see you when you bring Patches in next week, and good luck with your games."

"Wait, and I'll walk you out." He followed her to the older model Honda parked next to his SUV. He hadn't enjoyed being with a woman this much in a long time. Suddenly, he couldn't wait to see her again.

∼

A WEEK LATER, Jimmy sat on one of the uncomfortable plastic chairs in the lobby of the emergency clinic. He had a snug hold on the leash while he and Patches waited their turn to see the doctor. According to Angela's definition, he could only describe the man sitting beside him as a James type. The guy wore an expensive gray suit, a light blue shirt, and a dark blue silk tie.

James looked down at his own clothes, faded denim jeans and a casual dark blue untucked shirt. His mouth turned up in a smile. Yeah, he was definitely a Jimmy.

"Do I know you?" The man said while leaning forward.

"I don't think so, or at least I don't recall meeting you."

The man was quiet for a minute and then said, "I know. Hometown boy. You're James Ross. The pitcher."

"Guilty as charged."

"You've come to the right place," He nodded toward Patches. "My girlfriend's the best."

"Your girlfriend?"

"Doctor Michaels. I think she's much too talented to waste her time here, but she says she needs the money to pay off her loans to start her own practice. I told her I'd bankroll her, but the lady is way too proud to take anything from me. Go figure."

"Yeah, go figure." Jimmy swallowed back his disappointment and felt a heavy, empty feeling invade his chest.

The man's voice rose as he continued to carry on about what should have been personal and private matters. "And even then, Angela wants to set up her practice in that God-forsaken neighborhood she lives in now. But she won't if I have anything to say about it."

Jimmy's thoughts swirled. Of course, Angela would have a boyfriend. A beautiful, intelligent woman like her wouldn't be single. But what was she doing with a world-class jerk like this guy?

CHAPTER 6

Angela opened the door to the waiting room and uttered an exasperated sigh when she saw Greg seated beside Jimmy with Patches at his feet. Now what? The argument they'd had again last night about her moving in with him hadn't ended well. She'd left the restaurant alone, refused to ride home with him, and called an Uber. Last night and this morning, she'd ignored his frequent calls, yet he there he was sitting next to Jimmy, for goodness' sake.

Then, this morning Angela's mother called her out of the blue. Angela had not heard from her in almost six months. Kathy was like a beautiful butterfly flitting from man to man. When the romance wilted, like it inevitably would, she would reappear in Angela's life along with her constant criticism and unsolicited advice until the next man came along. The combination of both situations left Angela emotionally exhausted.

Greg jumped up and rushed toward her. She stepped back to let him in and quickly closed the door behind her. "I am at work. How would you like it if I barged into your office in the middle of the day?" Her hands curled into fists as she tried to control her sudden spurt of anger. Sometimes she felt as if she had no control over her life.

"I don't want to talk to you, Greg. Please leave now." She spoke through gritted teeth and kept her voice low, but even so, she could see the staff gawking at them.

"I need to apologize, and I wanted to make sure you got the jumbo bouquet of roses and the card." He moved in for a kiss, but she turned her face away.

The flowers were so extravagant they almost covered my whole desk, she thought. "Yes, I got them. Please, can we talk later when I get off work? I am asking you to leave."

He turned, glanced around him, and plastered a big smile on his face as he opened the door. Then, as if making an announcement to the entire office, he said, "Of course, sweetheart. I'll see you tonight." Then, he strutted past Jimmy and Patches as if he hadn't a care in the world.

Angela straightened her back and pasted on a smile as she watched him leave. Then she looked around the waiting room where a few people sat holding their dog's leashes and said, "Hi, Jimmy. Come on back." He looked handsome as usual, and she felt that dizzying current she felt whenever she looked at him.

"Thank you, Doctor Michaels," he said, following her into the exam room.

She assumed he used her formal title for the benefit of anyone listening, but she didn't care if the others knew they were friends.

"You can lift Patches up on the table, and I'll check her out." She adjusted the stethoscope hanging around her neck. "Have you found a regular vet? She'll need to be spayed before she comes into her first heat."

"Yeah, I have an appointment set up for next week."

Angela examined the injured leg and then scratched Patches under her chin. "She's doing great, and the cast should come off in four more weeks. It's okay if she walks on the cast if she doesn't run or jump. And remember to keep her on a leash and kenneled if possible."

"I'll remember," he said. His voice sounded cold and formal.

Angela looked at him across the steel table, but he didn't meet her eyes and seemed preoccupied with Patches. Had she done something wrong? Had she misjudged him? Maybe he was a moody ass.

"Did I do something to upset you?" Just then, she thought about where Greg had been sitting in the waiting room. "Did Greg say something about me that upset you?" She cleared her throat and made him meet her eyes. "I don't talk about the animals or their owners to anyone outside this office. Did Greg say I told him something about you?"

"No, his conversation revolved around the two of you. I don't think he gave a thought to Patches or me." He lifted Patches down from the exam table and turned to go. "Thanks for taking good care of her, Doctor."

He was out the door and out of sight before she could say another word.

∼

JIMMY GOT in the car and slammed the door a little too hard since Patches whined from her cage in the back. "Sorry, girl. I'm a little pissed off, Okay?" He ran his hand through his short hair and looked at his face in the mirror. *Man, am I a poor judge of character or what?*

Last week in the coffee shop, he'd flirted with her, and damn it, she'd flirted right back. Yet, all the time, she'd been hooked up with that A-hole Greg. His thoughts raced. *Maybe I've been out of the dating game so long I don't know how to* act. *Perhaps she wasn't flirting with me at all. Maybe she touched my hand because she felt sorry for me.*

Well, he didn't need or want her pity. They were friends, that's all, and he had misconstrued the entire morning. He was an idiot to think she liked him. He was probably ten years older than she was, and he had a kid to boot. Angela was young and just starting her career as his was ending.

Man, he hadn't thought of himself as old, but he sure felt that way right now. Most of all, he was embarrassed. It wasn't often he made a complete fool of himself. Thankfully, he would never have to see her again. But he knew he wanted to.

When he'd met Cindy, everything had been so easy. They had both been in college working toward their own goals, and she was pretty, intelligent, and ambitious. He'd come from a working-class family, and she'd come from the country club crowd, but after her parents overcame the shock, they accepted him. Especially after a year in the minors, they brought him up to pitch for San Diego and offered a very lucrative contract.

He parked in the driveway of his parents' house, a tan stucco with lush green grass and palm trees growing in the decorative landscape rocks leading toward the backyard. He'd grown up in this house and walked the six blocks to school with his older brother.

Sam lived in Oregon now and was a financial planner. Jimmy had thought that the job would be exceedingly dull, but because Sam had dollars and cents tattooed on his eyelids, it was a perfect fit. Sam was also managing Jimmy's money and making a nice bundle for Jimmy's retirement.

Jimmy walked around to lift Patches out of the cage in the back and snapped on the leash. "Be on your best behavior, you hear? And that means no chasing the cats."

His mother met him at the door, hugged him, and leaned

down to pet Patches. "The cats scattered as soon as they heard Patches. Why don't you put her in the backyard and let her run around for a while?"

"Sorry, no can do, yet. She's not supposed to run or jump. I'll keep her here with me, if you don't mind."

"That's fine. Come on in, and I'll get you something to eat and drink. It's lunchtime."

They had remodeled the kitchen after he left for college, and it was bright and sunny. His dad, who was still working as an electrician, knew all the best guys in the local construction world, and they'd done a beautiful job. His mom had worked at various part-time jobs, but she had always been here when her boys got home from school, and she drove them to every baseball practice along with most of their friends.

"So, what's on your mind?" She gave him a knowing look. Sandra Ross was a handsome woman with short dark hair and intelligent light green eyes. Although short, she had a trim build. She barely reached his shoulder.

"Do I need a reason to visit my mother?"

"Considering that you just saw me two days ago, yes. Everything is okay with Matt, right?"

"As far as I know, he's at school and doing fine. I need some advice."

"Oh, well, sure. What's up?" As she listened, she busied herself, pulling lunch meat, lettuce, and tomatoes from the refrigerator and setting a bottle of cold water in front of him and a bowl of water on the floor for Patches.

"I met this woman. As you know, I've hardly dated at all, much less really liked anyone since Cindy died."

"I feel as if there's a but coming."

"She has a boyfriend. An obnoxious jerk, but still a boyfriend."

"That certainly is a complication, but it's better than her

having a husband," she laughed. "How do you know she has a boyfriend?"

"I took Patches into the emergency clinic to check her leg, and I happened to sit next to the guy in the waiting room. He couldn't stop yapping on and on about her being his girlfriend, so when I saw her, I was a complete ass."

"This woman works at the vet's office. Is that what you're telling me?"

"Angela is the veterinarian who fixed up Patches the night of the accident, and then I saw her again when I took Patches to board her at Hollywood's Kennel."

"Have you told her how you feel?"

"Well, no, because I don't know how I feel. Angela is smart, sweet, pretty, and the best part is Matt likes her too."

"Have you ever thought about talking to this Angela? Asking her if she has a boyfriend? Maybe she and this guy aren't serious. Maybe she dates other men. You said he's obnoxious. If she's as great as you say, I doubt she's making long-term plans with him."

She set the plate with a sandwich and chips in front of him and patted his shoulder. "Talk to her. If she's worth her salt, she'll be honest with you, and if she shuts you down, then nothing lost, nothing gained."

CHAPTER 7

Angela hated confrontations. For most of her life, she'd tried to go along to get along. While Angela was growing up, her mother stressed that looks were more important than brains. She told her daughter to use her beauty to get ahead, just like she had. Since her mother looked like a fifty-year-old Barbie Doll, and the men who circled around her didn't stay long, Angela had no intention of taking her mother's advice.

When Angela was fourteen, she met Dean Skully, a handsome boy with dark hair and chocolate eyes. Dean was the first to tell her she was intelligent and beautiful, and he liked her looks, but he loved her brains. He'd grown up in foster care and was street smart but also wickedly book smart. He loved all things, especially animals, and was determined to get a scholarship and become a veterinarian. When she lost him, she thought she would die and had loved no one since.

A confrontation with Greg was inevitable. She knew it was way past time. When the doorbell rang, she caressed the silver charm she always wore around her neck, tucked it beneath her blouse, and plastered on a smile.

Greg greeted her with another arm full of flowers. She wondered why some men thought flowers would automatically fix everything. Trying to hide her irritation, she thanked him and placed them on the breakfast bar in the kitchen.

"I see you're still mad at me." He sounded annoyed.

"I'm not mad, Greg, but I am disappointed. You humiliated me by talking to a stranger about our relationship at my place of business. You're pressuring me into doing something I am not comfortable with."

His voice hardened. "But moving in together is the next step in our relationship, and this place is a shithole."

When he saw her eyes widen in surprise at his rude words, he stopped and gentled his tone. "I love you, Angela. I want to take care of you." He moved toward her, and she took a step back.

"I can take care of myself, and I don't want to live with you. I'm fond of you, and we've had fun, but that's as far as it goes."

"But I love you, and I just assumed that you felt the same way. Is it marriage you want? We can do that, I guess. I thought that a proposal now would be too soon."

"I don't want to marry you. I don't want to hurt you either, but this relationship isn't going to work. We are too different. I grew up with a controlling mother, and the last thing I want is a controlling husband. I can see the handwriting on the wall when I'm with you. I want to be free to make my own decisions. Whether good or bad, they will be mine."

"You're breaking up with me?" His voice rose as if he couldn't believe what she said.

"Yes, and I know what a proud man you are, so it's fine if you tell all your friends that you broke up with me. Give them whatever reason you want, and I'll affirm it if I run into any of them."

Sudden anger lit his eyes. "You're crazy, You know that? You're damn right I'll tell everyone I broke up with you. Because I am. Right now. I gave you everything, and you threw it back in my face. I'm way too good for you." His face turned tomato red as he grabbed the flowers, turned, and stormed out the door.

Well, that went as well as I expected, she thought. As soon as his car was gone, she grabbed her backpack and was out the door. She felt lighter than she had in a long time.

∽

JIMMY SAT with Matt in a booth at the busy coffee shop close to Hollywood's Kennel. They decided to have breakfast after he'd stopped by early that morning to introduce Hollywood to his son. He had a couple of hours left before heading to the ballpark.

Matt had been excited to see all the different breeds and sizes of dogs and to play with them in the large exercise yard. He was very good with animals, and in the short time they'd had Patches, he'd taught her to sit and stay.

"Did you used to play with the dogs, Dad?"

"No, I was high school age when her son Shane and I were friends. We were much too mature for that." His lips turned up teasingly as he reached over and tousled Matt's curly hair.

He looked past Matt and saw Angela walk in. Her dark hair hung loose again, and she wore jeans and a blue and red checkered blouse. There it was, that attraction that he'd tried hard to fight that seemed to pull him toward her. She was a classic beauty who easily turned men's heads. He hadn't felt like this in a long time, and he'd been an idiot to push her away. So what if she had a boyfriend? Just like his mother said, that didn't have to be a permanent situation. Maybe he could make her take a second look at him if he played his cards right.

"What are you looking at?" Matt said, turning his head around and getting on his knees. "Look, Dad, it's Doctor Michaels," he announced in an exuberant voice.

"Well, it sure is," Jimmy said, sounding not nearly as surprised as he was.

Matt waved his arms and shouted, "Doctor Michaels, it's Matt."

She looked up, waved back, and gave Matt a bright smile as she made her way toward their table. "Do you want to sit down with me and Dad?"

Jimmy realized what a jackass he'd been at her office and quickly said, "Please sit down with us, Angela." He hoped by using her first name, she'd realize it was his way of apologizing.

"Oh, I was just getting coffee on my way to Hollywood's place. I really can't stay."

"Then please let me buy your coffee as an apology."

Matt looked confused. "What'd you do, Dad?"

"I was a grump the other day in her office when I took Patches in for her checkup. I wasn't very nice." He stood and looked into Angela's eyes as he said, "I'm very sorry."

"It's fine. Everyone has a bad day. I accept your apology." She looked at Matt, whose eyes were bright with anticipation, and she scooted in beside him.

"Your dad says you're feeling better. That's great."

"Yeah, I'm okay. Not a hundred percent, but okay."

Angela looked across the table at Jimmy and raised one eyebrow as if to say, *Are you listening to this kid?*

"Where'd you come up with that one?" his father said.

"From you. You say that a lot."

Jimmy smiled and said, "You're right. I probably do. Does that mean you're still feeling bad?"

"Sometimes I still get stomachaches, and I'm tired, but not all the time. I don't want you to worry." He turned toward Angela and said, "Since it's Saturday, my grandma and grandpa will take me to Dad's game tonight. Why don't you come?"

She looked at Jimmy, and he nodded his head in agreement. "I can leave you a ticket at the window if you want to come. I don't even know if you like baseball. Do you?"

A brief cloud passed across her eyes as she said, "Not in a long time, but I'd like to see you play."

"This will be the last game I pitch, so there will be a little celebration. Especially if we win. I'd like it if you were there."

She reached up and clutched the charm on her necklace and said, "Let me see if I can get someone to cover my shift."

CHAPTER 8

Angela had only been to the ballpark once years ago with Dean before either was old enough to drive. He had saved money from doing yard work, and they took the bus to downtown San Diego and sat in the cheap seats at the stadium. Funny, she should think of that now. Jimmy's invitation to the game had brought back a memory she had long ago tucked away in her mind.

She questioned why she was here. Was it because she was drawn to Jimmy Ross, the man, not the baseball player? A man who loved his son enough to take in a stray dog when he could have easily written a check to take care of all the animal's medical bills and calmly walked away.

Jimmy Ross poked at places in her heart she'd sealed off long ago and wasn't sure she wanted to open again. And then, there was young Matt, the motherless boy with big chocolate eyes, who made her want to wrap him up in her arms and cry for the losses they had both suffered.

As she strode up the path to the ballpark to pick up her ticket, she remembered how awestruck she'd been the last time she'd visited the outdoor facility and seen its majestic palm trees lining the perimeter. Then, she recalled that a breathtaking view of the downtown skyline on one side and the Pacific Ocean on the other awaited her when she reached the inside.

The day was cloudy with a cool breeze, and she was glad she'd thought to bring a windbreaker. She had arrived early because Jimmy said they would hold the retirement ceremony before the game.

An overweight usher with a generous smile helped her find her seat, and she immediately spotted Matt, who was looking around, jumping, and waving excitedly when he noticed her. The smile on his face reinforced her decision to come.

The boy was pure joy to be around and always seemed happy. He was sitting with an attractive dark-haired older woman and a man wearing a ball cap. Angela assumed they were Matt's grandparents. They had great seats in the infield section between home plate and first base on the lower level. When the man turned toward her, she could see his resemblance to Jimmy.

When she reached them, they both stood, and the woman said, "You must be Doctor Michaels. I'm Jimmy's mother, Sandra, and this is his father, Larry."

"It's a pleasure to meet you," Larry said. His voice was low and sounded very much like his son's.

"Please, call me Angela; the pleasure is mine." She turned to Matt and said, "Thank you for inviting me. I haven't been to a ballgame in years, and I had forgotten how beautiful this stadium is."

"Do you follow baseball?" Larry asked her.

"No, I'm sorry to say, I don't, but I attended my high school games." She smiled apologetically. "But, of course, that's not the same thing as the major leagues."

"Well, we're happy you came tonight. Matt was hoping you'd make it."

"I had to find someone to cover my shift. Thankfully, a colleague was willing to trade with me for next Saturday. I understand there is going to be a tribute to Jimmy."

"Jimmy?" Sandra said with a bright smile.

"Yes. We had quite a discussion about my using the name James or Jimmy when we first met, and we both decided he is a Jimmy. Isn't that what you call him? I thought that's what he told me."

"It is indeed. He was always called Jimmy until he went away to college." She turned to her husband and said, "I like this girl."

A woman appeared wearing a shirt imprinted with the team logo and a bright smile. "I'm here to escort Mr. and Mrs. Ross and Matt down to the field for the ceremony."

Sandra turned to Angela and said, "Come on, dear, I'm sure Jimmy would want you there."

"No, but thank you. This is a special moment for your family. I'll be fine watching from here."

A tribute from the beginning of Jimmy's career to the present flashed a montage of photos on the jumbo screens. Angela could see what he had looked like as a young man starting out and the various awards he had received over the years. She searched for a resemblance between a young Jimmy and Matt but found none except for the dark hair. The boy must take after his mother, she thought.

As he stood on the pitcher's mound, they presented Jimmy with a plaque, other presents, and several verbal tributes. Finally, they introduced his parents and son. When the game began, Matt got to throw out the first pitch, which was a good one right over home plate. Angela clapped and yelled, marveling at how Matt was a chip off the old block.

After the ceremony, Jimmy took the mound, Jimmy's

family returned to their seats, and Angela settled down next to them to watch the game. Sandra leaned in and said, "Jimmy told me you saved Patches after his car hit her."

"Yes, he and Matt brought her into the emergency clinic, but I wouldn't say I saved her life. She was in shock and had a broken leg, but thankfully, no internal injuries."

"Matt adores that dog, and he's fond of you, too. Do you have children?"

Angela answered quickly with her automatic reply whenever someone asked her that question. "No pitter-patter of little feet in my home, not even a cat or a dog."

"Oh my! I thought all vets had a menagerie. We have very spoiled cats."

"Believe me, if I could, I would. But I work long hours at the emergency clinic, and we cannot bring our pets to work. Right now, it wouldn't be fair to leave an animal alone all day and night, but it's something I will do when I get my own business or get better hours."

"You can come to visit Patches," Matt said. "She's really smart. I've always wanted a dog too, but we had the same problem because Dad was gone a lot, and when Mom was alive, she was allergic."

Marveling at the boy's grown-up attitude, she said, "Thank you, Matt. Maybe I'll do that sometime."

Larry nudged his wife and said, "I'm hungry. I'm gonna take Matt to get a hotdog. Can I get you gals anything?"

Angela felt her stomach growl at the mention of food. She was hungry. She'd been busy and had eaten nothing since her bowl of cereal that morning. "A hotdog sounds great to me."

She reached for her purse, and Larry said, "My treat."

"And how about you, my love?" he said to his wife.

"Same for me, and a bottle of water."

Larry and Matt slowly made their way down the steps. As

soon as they were out of earshot, Sandra said, "I'm going to be blunt if that's okay with you? I'm too old to play games."

"Uh, yeah, sure," Angela answered, a little bewildered. Had she done or said something wrong?

"Matt's quite smitten with you, and I don't want him to get hurt."

Angela was confused and wounded by the turn of the conversation. She tried not to show her discomfort. "Why in the world would I want to hurt Matt? He's adorable. Special."

"He misses having a mother, and I think he's trying to push you into a relationship with his father. I understand you're in a serious relationship with someone else."

Angela laughed. She couldn't help herself. "So that's why Matt invited me to the game. I guess Jimmy had no choice and had to leave me a ticket then. I had no idea. I'm not around children that much."

"You couldn't tell it by the way you interact with him. You'd make a good mother."

Angela looked away and tried to compose herself before she said, "I don't know what your son has told you or even why he was discussing me at all, but I'm not in a relationship with anyone anymore. I was dating a man for the last couple of months, but we broke it off."

"Because of Jimmy?" she blurted out.

Goodness, this woman was blunt. Angela realized nothing would do but to tell the truth. "No, or at least I don't think so. I didn't like it when my ex felt he could discuss our relationship with Jimmy, who was merely a stranger to him in the waiting room and say things that weren't true. Jimmy and I are just friends."

"Well then," Sandra said, giving Angela a broad smile, "That's all I wanted to know. I'm a nosy mother, and it's none of my business, but just because my son is almost forty doesn't mean I'm any less of a mother bear. Jimmy hasn't been interested in a woman since Cindy died, but I can see that he likes you. For what it's worth, I do too." She gave Angela a satisfied smile.

CHAPTER 9

*D*ressed in casual clothes and freshly showered, Jimmy greeted them with his dark hair still damp. Looking at him set off a fluttering feeling in the pit of Angela's stomach. He was such a gorgeous man and a talented athlete. But he was so much more. He was also a good father and son. She didn't want to look too closely because everyone had faults, and she didn't want to find his, or at least not yet. She needed for him to remain perfect, for the short term, at least.

The short term was as long as this would last. She would not allow her heart to be broken by a handsome hunk again. The last time she'd loved someone, she had struggled to survive the heartbreak.

From the moment she met Greg, she had known her feelings would remain superficial, but that was not the case with her initial feelings for Jimmy.

She blinked out of her thoughts when Jimmy said her name. "Angela, would you like to join us? Just for a little after the game celebration."

"Uh, I...."

Matt's voice chirped. "I've been before, and it'll be fun. Grandma and Grandpa are going to go. You'll like it."

"We'll go for a little while, and then we'll take you home to bed," said Sandra. "Your dad can pick you up in the morning. I'm sure he wants to stay awhile since this will be his last time with his friends after winning a game."

Angela looked at her watch and decided she could sleep when she was old, even if she had to go dragging into work tomorrow. "Sure, tell me where I'm going, and I'll meet you there."

"We're walking, my dear," Jimmy's mother said. "It's only a few blocks from here." Sandra slipped her arm through Angela's, and the older woman took off briskly with the rest of her family trailing along as she chatted about the game and her memories of Jimmy. Angela couldn't help but smile while thinking how wonderful it must have been to grow up in such a loving family.

When they approached a sizeable wooden door outside the pub aptly named *The Dugout,* Jimmy held it open when she walked through, giving her a generous smile as she passed him. The place was rowdy and overflowing with San Diego baseball caps and half-drunk patrons.

While Jimmy dutifully spent the next twenty minutes signing hats or baseballs, Larry and Sandra pulled her away to the dartboard. Angela turned out to be pretty good at throwing darts, which surprised them, but Matt, with a pitching arm like his dad's, was better.

Jimmy finally finished talking to his fans and approached them with several athletic-looking men. "Hey guys," he said as his eyes traveled over his parents and son while holding Angela's gaze. "These are some of my teammates. These folks are my mom and dad, and you all know Matt. And this is Angela Michaels."

Everyone shook hands, and Angela wondered what he'd

told them about her. A waiter showed them all to several large wooden tables put together in a separate room. As wives or girlfriends joined his friends, Angela knew she would never remember all the names.

As the evening wore on, she could hear the now-muted music from the main room and the buzz of conversation around her. When she had almost finished her beer, Jimmy sat down beside her. "Thank you for being here. I have to admit it surprised me to see you. I didn't think you'd come."

"Why not? You invited me, or at least you left me a ticket. Was that because of Matt?"

"Yes, and no. Matt likes you, so yes, it was because of him. But it was also for me; I like you too."

Just then, Sandra put her hand on Jimmy's shoulder and said, "Your father and I are leaving now. It's getting late, and Matt's worn out." His mother had a worried look in her eyes, and Angela hoped it wasn't because of her.

Angela looked at the boy. His eyelids drooped as he frowned at his grandmother. "I'm okay. I'm not too tired," but Angela could see he was.

"You know what, it is getting late, and tomorrow is just another workday for me, Sunday, or no Sunday. I'll walk back with you," Angela said.

"No," Matt's eyes were suddenly round and attentive. "You stay and keep Dad company, so he won't be all by himself. Maybe you can come over sometime and see how Patches is doing."

She flashed him a brilliant smile. "Maybe I will."

After Matt took his grandmother's hand and left the room, Angela said, "You've raised such a great kid. You must be very proud."

"I am, but believe me, he's not always the angel he appears to be around you. He has his moments. I've had plenty of help since my wife died. My parents are a godsend, and even Cindy's parents have helped a lot."

Angela raised an eyebrow. "Is there a story there?"

"Don't get me wrong, they're great people, but they just don't live in the real world. They've always had money and lived like it. I want Matt to appreciate and work for what he gets in life." He raked his fingers through his hair, saying, "I have no financial concerns now because I have invested my money well, but it hasn't always been that way."

She kept looking at him with rapt attention, finding it hard to look away. He drummed his fingers on the table, leaned back, crossed his arms, and frowned. "See there, you're doing it again."

"What?" she said with wide-eyed innocence.

"Letting me monopolize the conversation. Tell me about you. How did you grow up? Where did you grow up? How did you end up a vet? I know absolutely nothing about you except that you have an obnoxious boyfriend named Greg."

"Greg is not my boyfriend, or at least not anymore. We decided it would be best if we ended things." She looked around the room to see that almost everyone had wandered off to play pool or darts, and they were alone in the room along with only one other couple.

"You mean you decided. The guy that talked to me in your waiting room was not about to end things."

She pressed her lips together, rested her chin in her hand, and said, "If you ever run into Greg, that will be his story. Don't blow it for him, okay. He's not a bad guy."

Jimmy laughed, saying, "I would have loved to be a fly on the wall for that conversation and don't change the subject. Tell me about you."

She pushed her hair back from her face and gave him a pointed look. "My life isn't nearly as interesting as yours. You're a famous ballplayer with lots of interesting stories to tell. I'm a simple girl that's never been outside of California. Not even for school. I'm ridiculously boring."

"No, nothing is boring about you, Angela Michaels. Why a veterinarian?"

"It was a dream I had growing up. I wanted to take care of animals, especially those whose owners struggled with the cost of caring for their pets. I will work at the emergency clinic until I save enough money to open my own business."

"School loans?"

"Fortunately, not as bad as it could be. I had several scholarships and didn't have to take out ridiculous loans. How about you?"

"I got a baseball scholarship, but not a full ride. Unlike football, a full ride for baseball is very rare. I worked in the off-season and during the summers to supplement my income and went to school here in town. I lived at home until my senior year. That's when I met Cindy." For a moment, he seemed lost in thought and then brightened and continued. "Have you ever been married?"

"No?"

"Engaged?"

"Yes." Her hand instinctively reached to clutch the charm she wore around her neck, always tucked beneath her blouse.

Jimmy took her hand and looked up at her face. His eyes were gentle and understanding. "Why do you always touch your necklace when you're nervous or don't want to answer a question?"

Angela loosened her hand, and Jimmy gently placed his fingers on her neck, moving them down to touch the charm. She could feel the rough calluses on his fingers from years of throwing a baseball, and as he moved closer, she could smell the fresh, clean scent of soap from his shower.

"It's an angel," he said as his breath touched her cheek. "Because of your name?"

Her throat was tight, and her eyes stung from unshed tears, but she managed to whisper, "Yes."

"You were engaged to the person who gave you this necklace." He no longer asked her questions but spoke as if he knew the story.

Again, all she could manage to say was, "Yes."

"What happened? Why didn't you get married?"

She dropped her lashes quickly to hide the hurt in her eyes. "He died."

CHAPTER 10

Whoa! Jimmy thought as he reached for the dregs of his beer and quickly swallowed to stall for time. Of all the words he had expected to hear, those were not the ones. He had speculated that maybe Angela's fiancé had dumped her for someone else. But come to think of it, why would anyone sane leave a lovely, intelligent woman like Angela? The guy would have to be crazy or abusive.

Jimmy knew he and Angela were members of the same sad club that came at an unbelievable price. Her boyfriend had died. He was at a loss, so he spoke his thoughts aloud. "I'm sorry. I don't know what to say."

"It was a long time ago, and I'm sorry I got so emotional. His name was Dean, and he was my first and only love." She gently touched the charm again and said, "He gave me this on my sixteenth birthday."

"How did he die?" Jimmy's voice was gentle.

"He was minding his own business while driving home from work, and a drunk driver ran a red light."

He put his arm around her and pulled her close. "I'm so

sorry. The hurt never goes away, I know. You always blame yourself a little. In my case, I wonder why I didn't insist that Cindy get a checkup. She always hated to go to the doctor. I should have pushed."

"Yeah, and Dean was coming to see me. If he'd been on the way to his house instead of mine, he wouldn't have been at that intersection." She paused and took a breath. "But what ifs can't change the past."

Angela rested her head against his shoulder, and the warmth of her petite body beside him felt good. She closed her eyes and sighed as he looked down at her lovely face. He could smell the floral scent of her shampoo in her silky, soft hair. It felt natural to hold her, and being around her was so easy.

"Tell me about Dean," he said, hoping she would finally confide in him about her past.

She looked up but continued to rest her head against him as she spoke softly. "He was a great guy. Kind and funny. He had every reason to be angry at the world and rebel, but he didn't. He was orphaned as a young child and raised in the foster care system. When he was twelve, the social worker placed him with the Morgans. They were a kind couple, and Dean was in a stable home for the first time. He blossomed there."

She sat up and smiled, saying, "He was wicked smart, and he was at the top of his class when I met him. He was a talented athlete, too. I used to go to his baseball games in high school."

"He sounds like a remarkable guy." Jimmy was trying hard not to be jealous of a dead man.

"Dean died when he was seventeen, so I don't know what kind of man he would have become, but I think he would have made a significant impact. He certainly did in my life. He's the reason I became a veterinarian."

ANGEL'S HEART

Several of his teammates interrupted their conversation with friendly shouts as they gathered in the doorway. "Come on, Jimmy. This is our last night. Come and have some fun. We've got a bet going on how many shots you can drink."

Jimmy had always been one of the guys, and after Cindy died, he became one of the last people to leave a celebration. It was different tonight. He felt torn between being with Angela or pleasing his friends.

He hated to end the conversation, especially since she had shared her story with him, but the look on her face showed the moment was over.

"Go have fun," she said, sounding sincere. "I need to get home, anyway."

"No," he insisted. "You're not walking back to your car by yourself. Give me thirty minutes, okay, and then we can leave."

He stood and pulled Angela up with him when he turned to his friends. "No way am I drinking more than one shot, but I'll play another game of darts or shuffleboard with you. Then I'm out of here."

"You're on," a tall man with a red beard said and then laughed. One of the younger guys slugged Jimmy on the arm and looked at Angela as he said, "You're a lucky SOB."

"Don't I know it?" Jimmy said as he took Angela's hand and led her towards the billiard tables in the bar's main room.

~

ANGELA FOUND a free high-backed chair at a table where some women she'd met earlier were sitting. She couldn't recall any names, but she smiled and ordered a Coke.

She could hear the jovial banter among the men and watched Jimmy down a shot of tequila chased by salt and lime, then grimace. He turned and grinned when he spotted her, and she waved back and smiled.

One woman scooted down the line of chairs and sat next to her. "Hi, I'm Milly Findlay. That big, loudmouthed redhead is my husband."

"Hi, Milly. Angela Michaels."

"Come on down here, kiddo, and sit with us. We can talk about those fools over there," she said, pointing at Jimmy and his friends. "How do you know James?"

"Believe it or not, I'm his veterinarian."

"I imagine that comes in handy, although I didn't know he had a dog. Cindy didn't care much for animals. She always said how much she hated her in-laws' cats."

Angela didn't rise to the bait, if that's what Milly was hoping for, and turned back to her glass and took a sip.

"This is the first time James has brought a date to one of his games. It's nice to see he's getting out there and dating again," a younger woman with a ponytail said.

Angela shook her head as she insisted, "Oh, we're not dating. We're only friends."

Milly patted Angela on the arm and said, "If you say so, sweetie. But I'm his friend, and he doesn't look at me the way he looks at you."

Feeling suddenly uncomfortable, Angela changed the subject. "Do you ladies come to all the home games?"

"Nah, not me," Milly said. "We've got three kids that keep me jumping, but I wanted to come to say goodbye to James. I mean, it's not like we'll never see him again, but you know how it is. He'll be retired and move on to other things."

"I guess I really don't. He seems too young to retire, but I guess he's considered old in the sports world."

"Yeah, he's lasted a lot longer than most pitchers. Baseball is a young man's game," said an attractive blonde with a curvy figure. "So, which animal clinic do you work at?"

"An emergency clinic in the southwest part of the city."

"That sounds exciting. What are some of the weirdest things you've seen?" asked Milly.

"I mostly deal with animals who have been in accidents or are seriously ill. Sometimes I must give the owners bad news, so some days can be a real downer. But then, at other times, I get to save an animal's life, and that's very satisfying."

"So, nothing weird, then?" Milly prompted her to continue.

"I've treated a snake with sand in its belly and a hamster whose teeth had grown so long they were touching the roof of his mouth. Nothing that weird yet. I mean, it's common for dogs to swallow many strange things."

"Yuck, a slimy snake," Milly said, clearly repulsed.

"I must admit, I'm not an expert on snakes, and I had to call a professor at my old university about that one, but we fixed it up and sent it home to slither another day."

"Hey," Jimmy said, suddenly appearing beside her. "Are you ready to go?"

"Sure." She turned to Milly and the other women and gave them a warm smile. "It's been great talking with all of you."

They smiled and nodded as Milly said, "Yeah, you too. Maybe we can get together sometime."

"I'd like that. Thanks."

She shivered as they walked out into the cool night air. Jimmy helped her put on her windbreaker and then put his arm around her, pulling her close while they ambled down the empty sidewalk.

"Did you have a good time?" he said.

"Sure. You have some nice friends."

"How about Milly? She didn't give you a hard time, did she?"

"No, not at all. Why would she?"

"Oh, I don't know. Cindy didn't like her very much. I believe she said Milly was too nosy."

"She asked a lot of questions, but nothing intrusive that made me uncomfortable. Mostly she asked about my work, and we talked about your retirement."

"I'm glad you came tonight and told me about Dean. It means a lot to me. From the moment I met you, I knew you were someone special. Your kindness and warmth were a blessing to Matt and me on a stressful night. How you were with my parents tonight, and the thoughtful way you always treat my son, makes me realize how much I want you in my life."

He stopped, pulled her closer, and lifted her chin as the streetlights illuminated his rugged face. "I really like you, Angela Michaels, and right now, I really need to kiss you."

Her mouth trembled, and her heart beat a staccato rhythm as she put her arms around his neck and stood on her tiptoes. He let his hand glide down her neck as his arms encircled her, and when he looked into her eyes, she saw passion and maybe even more in his tender expression.

The expectation was torture, and she felt her knees weaken as his mouth descended. She felt warm and safe as well as vulnerable. Then his lips met hers hesitantly at first, and then his mouth covered hers hungrily. She gave herself freely to the passion of his kiss and surrendered to all the feelings and desires she'd kept hidden for so many years, offering them now to this extraordinary man.

CHAPTER 11

The following day when she woke up, Angela opened her eyes and felt like she was floating on clouds. She touched her lips, remembering the kiss they'd shared. Ending the evening with just one kiss had been difficult, but she feared where it might lead. She wasn't sure if she was ready for what came next.

Knowing that Jimmy was a man she could easily fall in love with scared her to death. Tucking her hair behind her ears and out of her eyes, she padded barefoot to the kitchen for her morning coffee.

A loud knock at her door startled her. Her first thought was of Jimmy, but she chided herself. It couldn't be him. He didn't even know where she lived. Standing on her tiptoes, she peered through the peephole and then frowned.

Conflicted, her thoughts raced. I'll pretend I'm not home. No, I can't do that. The woman standing there is my mother, after all, even if she is a poor excuse for one. Angela opened the door and stepped back as Kathy pushed her way into the house.

"Why you live in this dump is beyond me, Angela. Some

lowlife could have accosted me while I was standing here on the stoop. You're a veterinarian, for heaven's sake, and you must make a bundle. Probably as much or more than a doctor."

Angela let her mother's critical tirade flow right over her. After all, she'd heard it all before. There was nothing wrong with her small house or her neighborhood. She shut the door and walked back toward her small kitchen, filled with the fragrant aroma of coffee. She was craving a cup of it now more than ever. It was true that a veterinarian could make a nice living, but her salary wasn't anywhere near as sizable as her mother thought.

"What are you doing here, Mother?" Her words held a strong suggestion of reproach.

"Well, it's nice to see you, too."

Angela took a sip of her coffee before saying, "I haven't spoken to you in months. Then you called and showed up in one week. What's going on?" She knew there had to be a reason for her mother to act so jittery.

With shaky hands, her mother took a cup from the rack on the kitchen counter and helped herself to the coffee. She looked for a spoon and added sugar before blurting out, "It's Raul. We had an argument. Can you imagine that? He wants to monopolize all my time. You know me, darling. I need to be free."

Yes, Angela thought, she could imagine it. Her mother's freedom usually came at the expense of everyone else around her. Along with being demanding and needy, her mother could also be devious.

Kathy's personality was so unstable it was impossible to predict which side of her one might see on any given day. As a young child, Angela and her mother had lived with her grandmother. She was happy there, and her life had a semblance of normalcy until her grandmother died.

Suddenly, it left Angela alone with her unstable mother, and her life became a series of crises that were seldom handled with maturity. Angela had to grow up way too fast. Somehow, Kathy had found the money to buy a new car and move them to a comfortable home. Angela did not know where her mother got the money and had often wondered.

Kathy was a good-looking woman with honey-blonde hair, hazel eyes, and a curvy figure. Her looks belied her age, and she never revealed to her many younger lovers that she was a mother with a grown daughter. Angela was born when Kathy was eighteen. If her mother knew who Angela's father was, she never revealed it.

While Angela was in college, Kathy married a wealthy man. Her mother walked away with a tidy sum when the marriage ended four years later.

"Sorry, Mother, but I never met Raul, so I can't really comment on what he would or wouldn't do."

Angela took a gulp of the hot coffee. She continued her usual morning routine as best she could while hoping to find the reason for the visit. "I've got to get ready for work. Can we continue this conversation later?" She took another sip and continued. "And why did you come by so early? Surely not to tell me about your boyfriend."

Kathy smirked. "One of my friends from the club called me last night and said they saw you. Did you go to a baseball game yesterday?"

"Why do you ask? If someone told you they saw me there, I obviously did."

"Well, it doesn't seem like you. I mean, you haven't been interested in sports since, well, since …"

"Since high school, Mother. Since Dean died. You can say his name."

"I don't like to bring up that boy. It's painful for all of us."

Angela snorted but let the comment pass. "Yes, I was at a

baseball game. Shock of all shocks. Why do you want to know?"

"My friend said you were with James Ross's family. I didn't know you were friends with them, that's all. I mean, you don't really have anything in common with them, do you?"

Angela rubbed her tired eyes. She was trying to be civil, but her mother wasn't making any sense. "I don't know them at all. In fact, last night was the first time I ever met them."

"Did you meet James Ross's wife and kids?"

"His wife died a few years ago, and he only has one son. Why the twenty questions?"

"Just curious. It's interesting that my daughter is hanging out with a celebrity." She took Angela's face between her hands and kissed her quickly. "Well, gotta run. I've probably let Raul stew long enough."

Angela plopped down on her kitchen chair and stared at the door, wondering what had just happened. Kathy had always been a little crazy, but she was teetering on the edge this morning. Something was going on. Her mother was freaking out, and it had something to do with Jimmy or his family, but what?

~

JIMMY WOKE up feeling a little unsettled. Two significant events in his life had occurred yesterday, and both left him elated and terrified. He had officially retired from baseball, which had dominated his every waking moment for over half of his life. His body was relieved, but his mind was conflicted. He had plenty of money and several business opportunities that would keep him busy until he was an old man, but the change would be an adjustment.

And then there was Angela Michaels, a delightful surprise

in his life. Jimmy hadn't expected the surge of desire that overtook him when he kissed her. He could sense that she felt the same way, but thankfully she'd had the sense to stop him from pulling her into her car and making mad passionate love to her. He'd felt like a hormonal teenager most of last night.

Remembering it this morning put a silly grin on his face. He let Patches out, slipped on shorts and running shoes, and reached for his phone before walking out the door for a morning jog. He texted his mother asking if Matt had made it to school okay and then sent a text to Angela, inviting her to lunch.

His mother answered immediately to say that she had dropped Matt off at school successfully and he would take the bus home. It disappointed him to get no response from Angela. He wanted more of what they had begun last night.

Halfway through his run, his phone rang, and relief washed over him when he saw it was Angela. When had he ever felt this way about a woman? He stopped, took big gulps of air to catch his breath, and answered.

"Hi," she said. "I'm sorry. I've been in surgery and just saw your text."

She sounded so damn sexy, and he could picture her in her white lab coat with her lush dark hair resting on her shoulders and remembered those magnetic eyes. He paused for a long moment before finally saying, "I'm out of breath. Running."

"Oh, sorry to bother you. I'll text and …."

"No," he interrupted quickly, "don't hang up. I'm good. Can you break away for lunch?"

"Yes, but probably not until about one. Will that be too late?"

Jimmy smiled as he wiped the sweat from his face and looked around his tree-lined neighborhood. He squinted into the bright sunlight of a beautiful September day. "No, that will work out great. I think I passed a park near the emergency clinic the other day. How about meeting me there, and I'll bring lunch? The day's too pretty to stay inside, and we won't have to deal with a crowded restaurant. How does that sound?"

"That sounds amazing. Why don't you bring Patches along, and I can check her out?"

"I can do that. Any foods you don't like?"

"Nope, I'm easy."

He laughed and said, "Easy, Doctor Michaels, is something you are not."

CHAPTER 12

Jimmy found a picnic table under a shady eucalyptus tree and set down the large paper bag and a small cooler. He looked around and saw a family with young children, an older man sitting on a park bench while tossing popcorn to the birds, and several people walking their dogs. Everyone was far enough away to provide plenty of privacy for them. He wanted to get to know her and speak freely without an audience.

He rubbed his hands together, looked around, and spotted Angela as she got out of her car. She waved and moved toward him on the freshly mown grass, and when she got close, he smiled, put his hands on her shoulders, and gently pulled her in for a kiss. It was much more than a friendly kiss, and when he moved away, he said, "It wasn't my imagination. Your lips are as soft as I remember."

Her face flushed bright red, and she tried to look around, but he held her still. "Nobody cares if I kiss you. I bet that old guy sitting on the bench is as jealous as hell."

"Are you always such a charmer, Mr. Ross?"

"Not usually," He grinned and the laugh lines around his eyes crinkled. "You hungry?"

"Starved. I didn't have breakfast because of a surprise visit from my mother."

He pulled two plastic cartons from an oversized brown paper bag and pointed to the cooler. "I brought water and Coke. I wasn't sure which one you preferred. There's a great sandwich place not too far from my house. You said you like everything, so I brought you a peanut butter and banana sandwich."

He looked at her confounded expression and burst out laughing. "Well, if it was good enough for Elvis, it should be good enough for you."

"Uh, well, uh, I never uh. …." she babbled before regaining her composure. "Okay, what the heck? That's great."

"You're so cute. It's chicken salad on sourdough, but if you're disappointed, I can go back and get the banana."

She slugged him on the arm, and this time, she laughed as he pulled her in for another kiss. Patches whined and pushed her nose between them and then gave a soft bark.

"I think she's jealous," Angela murmured against his lips.

They broke apart, and Jimmy shook his finger at the dog. "You have to wait your turn. You'll get your kiss in a minute."

Angela bent down and stroked Patches between the ears, saying, "You're looking good, pretty girl. I'm not trying to hurt your guy, I promise." She gave Patches a quick once over and then squeezed sanitizer from a plastic bottle in her bag to clean her hands. "Her leg is looking good. You and Matt are doing a great job."

Jimmy tossed Patches a Kong filled with cheese and wrapped the leash around the table leg as he said to Angela, "You ready to eat?"

"You bet." She pulled a water bottle from the cooler and sat across the table from him. "It is so thoughtful of you to bring me lunch. I usually settle for whatever I can scrounge from my fridge."

"And what did you scrounge today?"

"A carton of yogurt and a baggie of crackers."

"Umm, yummy," he teased in mock horror. "You said you got a surprise visit from your mother. That's not a good thing?"

"Uh, no. A visit from Kathy, especially early in the morning, is never a good thing. She usually has an ulterior motive."

"I take it you two are not close," he said, sipping his water. He couldn't imagine not being close to his mother. He'd always been able to confide in her.

"My mother was young when she had me, and my grandmother mostly raised me until I was about fourteen. When she died, life was challenging."

"How about your father?"

"Don't know. Never met him, and there wasn't a father listed on my birth certificate." She gave him a soft smile and said, "I'm not exactly the girl next door, Jimmy."

"You are to me. Who your parents are has nothing to do with how I feel about you." He reached for her hand and gently entwined their fingers. "Look at you. You're a successful professional and a sweet, caring woman. You managed that all on your own."

"I wasn't totally on my own. I met Dean after my grandmother died, and he was the best thing that ever happened to me. Although he had absolutely no material possessions, he gave me hope and confidence every day. He's the one that wanted to be a vet. He talked about how animals never judge people. All they want is to give and receive love."

"I think that's what most people want too. So, when he died, you decided to become a vet in his place?"

"Not exactly. We talked about going to school and then

opening a practice together in a disadvantaged neighborhood to help low-income people afford pet care. It was a pleasant dream, but who knows if it would have happened? Things come along and complicate or change dreams."

She picked at her sandwich, and a wistful smile crossed her face. Jimmy wondered if talking about Dean had made her sad. He never wanted this lovely woman to be sad.

"I graduated from high school early, and Hollywood helped me apply for scholarships and grants. After I left for school, my mother and I drifted farther apart, not that we were ever close. When she comes around, she usually wants something, but this time I can't figure out what it is."

Angela finished her lunch and deposited her carton and empty water bottle in the trash. "She was overly curious that I had gone to the baseball game last night and sat with your family. Her name was Kathy Germaine or Kathy Michaels before she married her ex-husband. Do you know her?"

He thought for a moment and then shook his head. "No, it doesn't sound familiar. Maybe I met her someplace, and I don't remember. What does she do?"

"She doesn't, unless you count playing golf and tennis, going to the gym, and hanging out with the right people. Her divorce left her well off, and that poor man still adores her. My mother is a beautiful woman with many male admirers."

"Doesn't sound like anyone my folks would know either, and my life with Cindy revolved around our careers and Matt. Cindy may have crossed paths with her, but I never heard her mention that name."

"Cindy was a lawyer, right?"

"She was, but she only worked part-time after Matt came along."

"And you?" she sat back down, and after tossing the restaurant bag, he swung his legs over the bench to sit beside her. "I'm not sure, but I don't think they let you major in baseball," Angela said.

"No, that would have been too easy. I was a business major."

"Good to know. When I start my business, I know who I'll contact for help."

"The emergency vet job isn't permanent for you?"

"No. Don't get me wrong, I enjoy it, but most stories don't end as happily as the one with you and Patches." The dog's ears picked up at the mention of her name, and she looked expectantly at Jimmy.

"Usually, I'm the bearer of bad news in the waiting room. The pay is excellent, and I can pay off my school expenses that weren't covered by scholarships or grants and then save up for my own practice. How about you now that you've hung up your glove?"

"I want to spend as much time as possible with Matt. He'll be thirteen soon. Before I know it, he'll leave home. Work-wise, I've got some endorsement offers, and I own some real estate in town. That should keep me busy."

Angela looked at her watch and said, "I've got to get back to work. This has been fun. Thank you."

They both stood, and as he looked at her lovely face, he knew exactly what he wanted, and he wanted Angela. "Do you think we could go on an actual date? Like dinner, maybe?"

"I'd like that. Let me check the clinic's calendar, and I'll let you know which night I'm free. My schedule changes constantly. One of the drawbacks of the job."

He tipped her chin up and gave her a soft kiss. "I'll wait to hear from you then." As he watched her walk to the car, his emotions were all over the place. What was he doing? Angela wasn't like the other women he'd been with since Cindy's death.

Being with Angela would have emotional consequences that he wasn't sure he was ready for, but he was helpless to resist her magnetic charms. Each time he saw her the pull was stronger, and she was completely unaware of how special she was.

CHAPTER 13

Angela pushed her dark hair back and smiled as she inhaled the lemon-scented furniture oil and surveyed her living room. Everything looked perfect. She had spent most of the morning cleaning and polishing her small two-bedroom, one-bathroom house until it shined.

She was usually a neat nick anyway, but she wanted to ensure her home would make a good impression tonight because she'd invited Jimmy over for dinner. The house was only a rental, but she was proud of it and took care of it as if it were her own.

To heck with what Greg and her mother thought of it. But she wondered if Jimmy would see it the same way. Maybe she was looking through rose-colored glasses, and the place really was a dump.

She took off her rubber gloves and deposited them in the trash. She thought, if Jimmy didn't like where she lived, then maybe he wasn't the guy for her, regardless of the heart palpitations she felt whenever she was with him. She knew who she was and wouldn't change for any man even if his kisses did make her weak in the knees.

She liked her neighborhood. The old couple who lived next door had raised four children and now had ten grandkids and three great-grandkids. Mr. Cook was a retired bus driver, and Mrs. Cook had worked in a school cafeteria. On the other side of her lived a young couple who were expecting a baby in a couple of months. The husband attended night school, and the wife worked at a big box store. Yes, there was some crime in the area, but there was crime everywhere. The neighborhood reminded her of her home when her grandmother was alive, and those were some of her happiest memories.

Angela had declined Jimmy's suggestion to go out to a restaurant for dinner and suggested that she cook for him instead. She imagined he didn't get many home-cooked meals because of being on the road so often. It didn't take any persuasion for him to agree. She'd bought wine and spent a fortune on two ribeye steaks at the meat market her neighbor had suggested.

Once she had prepped the food, she switched to white capris, a flashy pink top, and open-toed sandals that flaunted her newly painted pink nails. She could feel butterflies beat their wings in a staccato rhythm in her stomach. What in the world? Why was she so nervous? It was only a date, and a casual one, at that.

But somehow, she knew it wasn't. It felt like much more than that. As her grandmother used to tell her, the heart knows what it knows. She had a feeling this night would be the beginning of something that might change her life.

Her doorbell rang, and when she opened it, there he was on her front porch with a crooked smile on his chiseled face and holding out a bouquet wrapped in tissue paper. She moved a step back to let him in, and he leaned down to brush his lips against hers in a soft kiss as he spoke. "You look amazing."

She smiled and looked him over from head to toe. "You look pretty good yourself." He had on worn denim jeans, a soft long-sleeve shirt with the sleeves rolled up, and brown chukka boots.

"The flowers are beautiful. Thank you." She moved to the kitchen and took a small clear glass vase from a cabinet. As she arranged the flowers, she looked over her shoulder and said, "Would you like to eat now, or do you want to have a glass of wine first?"

"What's for dinner?"

"Ribeyes, salad, and baked potatoes. I thought that was a safe bet since most guys like a good steak."

"And you can cook a good steak?"

"I learned from the best, my grandmother. There wasn't anything that woman couldn't cook."

"Let's have wine first," he said, lifting a bottle of red wine from the counter. Earlier, she had opened it to let it breathe and set out two glasses. He poured a glass for each of them, and they clinked glasses, and both said, "Cheers," at the exact moment which made them smile.

She led him outside to the small wooden patio with a pergola overhead covered in ornamental grapevine. "Did you do all this?"

"The patio was already here, but I put up the pergola and planted the grapevine. Soon the leaves will change to a colorful, deep red." She sat on one of the bright turquoise cushions on the small wicker loveseat and patted the seat next to her. He settled beside her and put his arm around her, pulling her close.

Angela sipped her wine and ran her finger around the rim of the glass. "Where is Matt tonight? You know you could have brought him with you."

"He went to a movie with my parents, and then he will spend the night. If he was with me, I wouldn't be able to do this," he said as he set his glass on a small table and kissed her tenderly, gently nibbling her lip before he moved away.

She paused a moment to savor the kiss before saying, "You're an amazing father, you know. Matt's a lucky boy."

His eyes became distant, and he didn't respond for the longest time. Finally, he said, "I was away from home a lot, and it was hard on both my wife and Matt. Besides her demanding job, she had to make most of the day-to-day life decisions, and she bore the greatest responsibility for our son."

Angela pushed her hair back from her face. "Granted, I don't know a lot about professional baseball, but surely you all were in a financial position to allow your wife and Matt to go with you, especially during the summer months and holidays."

"That's what I thought, but she was adamant that Matt have a normal life and not live out of hotel rooms. Before Matt, she was consumed with having a baby. When we finally got him, she became a totally devoted mother and involved herself in every aspect of his life."

"And that was a bad thing?"

"Yes, he didn't have room to grow into his own person. She hovered over his every decision. We fought about that and about the amount of time I was away from home."

"I'm sorry, Jimmy. That must have been hard for you, and it created an unbelievable position for you to be in."

"If I'd been home, things might have been different. Cindy started an affair with one of Matt's teachers. When I found out, she ended it, and we went to counseling. It helped us both, and things were good again before she died. But it took me a while because once you lose trust in someone, it's hard to get it back."

Angela took a sip of her wine and thought about what he said. She wanted to tell him about what she had gone through as a teenager since he had just unburdened himself to her, but she was afraid of what he would think. The last thing she wanted to see was pity or rejection in his eyes, but she knew she would have to tell him soon if they were to have a meaningful relationship.

Jimmy put his wineglass on the small table and said, "On a lighter note, I think it's time we talked about something besides me and my woebegone past. In fact," he continued in an upbeat tone, "I would much rather talk about you. I've been looking forward to having some alone time with you since the night we met."

She felt a little lightheaded from the wine, and when she glanced at him, his smoldering eyes never looked away from her face. His movements were slow and easy as his large, calloused hands moved to her shoulders and turned her body toward him. He gently raised her chin, and she felt lost in those pale green eyes flecked with gold.

Then he kissed her forehead, and his lips trailed down to shower kisses around her lips and along her jaw. Suddenly her arms were around his neck as he pulled her closer, so close she didn't think she could take another breath. His manly scent evoked sweet sensations as she melted into his muscular arms.

"You're not going to tell me it's too soon, are you?" His voice was a husky whisper. "Please don't say that. Being near you like this is driving me crazy."

She forgot about the steaks in the fridge and the baked potatoes warming in the oven when she said, "No, I will not tell you that. Please don't stop."

His touch was fiery but gentle as his hand moved beneath her blouse and cupped her breast. She was glad now that she'd worn the sexy underwear she'd bought on a whim several days earlier that mocked her every time she opened her drawer. Was it in anticipation of this very moment?

She pulled his tucked-in shirt free and ran her hands up his warm back, massaging his firm muscles with her small fingers. She heard his erratic breathing and basked in the knowledge of her power over this strong, beautiful man. "I have a comfortable bed, Jimmy, unless you'd rather continue to make out like teenagers on the back porch," she giggled.

"When I'm with you, Angel, I feel like one." He scooped her up in his arms like a scene from a romantic movie and said, "Point me toward this comfortable bed."

∼

"Hungry?" She asked playfully many hours later while lying in his arms, with only the sheet covering them.

He turned his head to face her and marveled at how she looked with her wild, dark hair tangled on the pillow. Her face looked smaller and more delicate without her glasses, although he enjoyed looking at her either way.

"Not right now, but give me a minute to recover, and I will be."

She burst out laughing. "Not that kind of hunger. I meant for steak, potatoes, and salad. I'm not sure if they're still edible, but I have a frozen pizza."

"I'm so sorry to have ruined your delicious dinner. I will make it up to you, I promise. I'm fine for now."

"You could stay for breakfast, and we could have steak and eggs."

"I wish I could stay, but I need to get home." He sat up and slid to the side of the bed. She watched him walk to the chair where he had tossed his clothes in a heap and begin to get dressed.

"I thought Matt was at his grandparents."

He detected a note of disappointment in her voice. "He is,

but I need to pick him up early. The reason I need to leave now is your fault."

She pushed herself up on her elbows. The sheet fell below her naked breasts, but she pulled it back up shyly. "My fault? What are you talking about?"

Too late, he realized his words had hurt her. He crossed the room in three strides, sat beside her, and kissed her devouringly. "I'm just teasing you, sweetheart. It's because you saved my dog. I need to rush home and let Patches out. She's been in the house all night."

CHAPTER 14

The following morning, Jimmy got up early, like he always did, took Patches outside, showered, and ate a quick breakfast consisting of a protein shake and muffin.

He watched the dog walk around the backyard, which brought Angela immediately to mind. Whenever he thought about her and their passionate love-making the night before, he couldn't help but smile. Jimmy knew he should take things slowly because he had Matt to consider, although that wasn't what he wanted.

He'd been on four other dates since Cindy's death, and all of them had been complete disasters. Being with Angela was a completely different experience. It had become serious so quickly that one or both could easily get hurt if things didn't work out, not to mention how it could screw up Matt. Jimmy was completely smitten with Angela, but his first concern was always about his son.

When he returned to the kitchen, his cell rang, and recognizing his mother's ringtone, he quickly answered, "Hey,

ANGEL'S HEART

Mom, what's up? I was just getting ready to head over and pick up Matt."

"That's what I'm calling about. He threw up his breakfast and said he felt horrible. He went back to bed, but I thought I should let you know so you could call the doctor."

"I'll call his office right now, but since it's Sunday, I'm sure I'll only get his answering service. The doctor's pretty good at getting right back to me."

∼

THIRTY MINUTES LATER, Jimmy sat on the bed in his mother's guest room while watching his son sleep. Matt's dark, curly hair was falling in his face. He was a good-looking kid and a good size for his age.

His mother came up behind Jimmy and put her hand on his shoulder. "I'm getting worried, Son," she said quietly. "This has been going on way too long, and when he wakes up, take a good look at his skin. He looks jaundiced to me. I'm not a doctor, but …."

"When did you notice that?" Jimmy interrupted. His voice was laced with alarm.

"This morning. When he got up, he said his stomach hurt and then threw up."

A few moments later, Jimmy answered his phone and explained Matt's symptoms to the pediatrician. After listening, he thanked the doctor and pocketed his phone. "Dr Brewer said to bring him in first thing in the morning unless he gets worse. If he does, he said to take Matt to the emergency room at Children's Hospital."

Jimmy rested his hand on Matt's forehead. He was relieved that the boy wasn't running a temperature, but he was still frightened and frustrated. Matt opened his eyes and smiled when he saw Jimmy. "Hey, Dad, when did you get here?"

"Hey, yourself. I've been here for about ten minutes. Your grandmother says you aren't feeling good."

"I'm not. I feel awful. I think I'm going to …." Then he leaned forward and vomited all over Jimmy.

∽

JIMMY HAD CHANGED into shorts and a T-shirt that he kept in the gym bag in his car, and now he was sitting in the hospital's waiting room with Matt's head resting in his lap. He filled out at least a million intake forms before he finally heard Matt's name called.

A nurse was checking Matt's blood pressure when a doctor entered the room and said, "Good morning." Then he scrolled on the screen of an iPad before looking directly at his patient. "Hello, Matt. I'm Doctor Wu. I understand your pediatrician recommended you come in because your symptoms have been going on for several weeks."

Jimmy liked the fact that the doctor was speaking directly to Matt.

"Yeah," Matt said. "I keep throwing up, and most of the time, I feel like I'm going to, even if I can't. It's getting kind of old. I'm sick of feeling sick."

"Why don't you lie back and let me take a look?"

Jimmy watched as the doctor slowly pressed on Matt's belly. When he touched the upper right portion above Matt's stomach, the boy flinched. "Does that hurt?"

"Yes," Matt said between clenched teeth. "A lot."

After he examined Matt's skin tone, he concentrated on his face and eyes. Then he turned to Jimmy. "When did Matt develop jaundice?"

"What's that?" Matt said. "What's jaundice?"

"We just noticed it this morning." Jimmy swallowed hard and said, "What's going on?" He looked at Matt and then back at the doctor. "Matt's almost thirteen. He's old enough to understand."

"I'm concerned about your liver, Matt. The jaundice or yellowing of the skin usually indicates a problem. Your liver has high bilirubin levels, and bile is secreting or leaking from your liver."

"That sounds yucky."

"What's causing it?" Jimmy said, as his thoughts raced in a dozen directions.

"We don't know yet. The first step is to draw some blood and see the actual numbers, take a urinalysis, and order an ultrasound or CT scan or both, depending on the test results."

"His pediatrician took blood last week and said everything looked good."

"He probably ordered a basic metabolic panel looking for infection. This time we'll look a little deeper."

Doctor Wu held out his arm and helped Matt to sit up. "It could be any number of things from a virus, an infection, or even an inflamed gallbladder, although at his age, that isn't likely." He looked at Jimmy and said, "We'll get to the bottom of this. I promise."

∼

JIMMY WAITED in the small ER waiting room while they took Matt to another hospital floor for an ultrasound and a CT scan. He spoke to his parents and promised to let them know as soon as he knew more. He thought about calling Angela just to hear her voice but knew that would be selfish. Why bring her into his troubles when he didn't have any answers?

He leaned back in his chair with his head against the wall

and closed his eyes. He must have fallen asleep because he jerked awake with the sound of the door opening. Matt, looking pale and weary, sat in a wheelchair as the hospital aide pushed him into the room.

"Hey, kiddo, how'd it go?"

"They put this slimy gunk on me and pressed down on my stomach. It hurt a little, and then they had me lie on a table and be still while they took pictures of my insides. I hope I get to see them. Especially the liver."

Jimmy laughed and looked away while blinking away threatening tears. "I'm sure you will."

"Can I have something to drink, or do you think I'll puke all over you again?"

"It comes with being a parent. It's not the first time you've puked all over me. You even did so at a restaurant when you were about two. Now that was gross. We'll ask the doctor when he comes back."

The door opened again, and Doctor Wu came in accompanied by an older woman wearing a lab coat. The doctor had hair streaked with gray and wore rimless glasses. Her no-nonsense demeanor made her an imposing figure although she was short. Something hardened in the pit of Jimmy's stomach because now he realized something was seriously wrong with his son.

"Mr. Ross, Matt, this is Doctor Heller, a hepatologist. In layman's terms, she is a liver specialist. She will review the results of the tests with you both and explain your options."

"Options?" Jimmy said while looking at the woman as he approached Matt and put his arm around him.

Doctor Heller held out her hand to both Jimmy and Matt. It's a pleasure to meet you both. I've looked at all the test results and scans, and I feel that time is of the essence. I'd like to admit Matt into the hospital today and perform a liver biopsy tomorrow morning."

ANGEL'S HEART

"Wait, Doctor Wu said we have options. What did he mean?"

"You could take Matt home and return in the morning, but I would prefer to start him on IV fluids since he is dehydrated, and I want to withhold food or liquids until after the biopsy. That would be more difficult at home," Doctor Heller said.

"What's a biopsy, Dad?" Matt's eyes filled with tears, and Jimmy hugged him tighter.

"It's when we take a small piece of tissue from your liver so we can look at it under a microscope," said Doctor Heller.

"Will it hurt?"

"Not during the procedure, but you'll be uncomfortable afterward for a few days."

"I don't think I want to do that. Can't you do some other test?"

Doctor Heller locked eyes with Jimmy, her face full of concern and compassion, and then she smiled. She was asking him for help, and he knew he had to step up and be an adult.

"Doctor Heller is saying this is the next step in finding out why you've been feeling bad for such a long time. They've done all the tests they can on the outside, and now they need to look inside. I'll be right here with you the whole time. I promise."

Matt nodded and seemed to accept his father's explanation. "I think we'll stay here tonight instead of going home," Jimmy said. "Would it be possible to get me a rollaway bed? Also, Matt says he's thirsty."

"After we get your saline IV going, you won't feel thirsty anymore, Matt. In the meantime, you can have a few ice chips. And tomorrow after the biopsy, you can have whatever you want to eat and drink."

Jimmy's throat was tight, but he had to hold himself

together and not show any emotion. He couldn't let Matt know how frightened he was.

CHAPTER 15

Closely followed by her husband of over forty years, Sandra Ross rushed down the hospital hallway. Jimmy stood in the doorway of Matt's room and watched as his parents presented a united front the same way they had after Cindy's death.

"Jimmy," his mother said, engulfing him in a tight, loving embrace. "What can we do?"

Larry stuck out his hand before pulling Jimmy into a hug. His father was a man of few words but had always supported and encouraged him in everything he did. He could only strive to be as great a parent as his mother and father were.

Jimmy rubbed his head and tried to locate a rational thought. His world was tilted sideways, and he didn't know how to right it. "I don't know. We won't know anything definite until after the biopsy, and the results won't come back until Tuesday or later."

"Did the doctors give you any idea of what they suspect?"

Jimmy looked back into Matt's room to make sure he was sleeping and would not hear the conversation. "It could be cirrhosis, hepatitis, or an infection. It could also be cancer or a bunch of other diseases that I can't pronounce."

Sandra gasped as tears sprang to her eyes. "Oh, no, Jimmy."

"We don't know anything yet, and Doctor Heller doesn't think cancer's what we're looking at. She advised me to stay off Google and wait until she has a diagnosis and a treatment plan."

"I think that's a wise decision. Have you called Chris and Ginger?"

He tried to suppress a frown and said, "No, I haven't done that yet. I thought I'd wait until I knew more."

"Hon, I know they can be difficult, but they love Matt, and since they're Cindy's parents, that makes them Matt's grandparents. too."

"I'm aware, Mom," he said.

"Your father and I will sit with Matt while you go downstairs and call them."

She patted his shoulder and gave him that motherly look even though he wasn't a kid anymore. He knew she was right. "Okay, I'll do that. Can I get you guys anything?"

"No, we're fine. What about Patches? Is she okay?"

"Ah, jeez, I haven't even thought about her. She needs to go outside. She's been locked up since this morning." He rubbed his head again and realized a splitting headache was forming between his eyes. He was exhausted from lack of sleep.

Then he thought about Angela. He knew he should call her, too, but what would he say? Who was he kidding? He avoided that conversation because he knew he'd fall apart if he talked to her.

He turned quickly and pushed open the door when he heard Matt's voice calling from inside the room. "Hey bud, look who's here. It's Grandma and Grandpa."

"Did you have a nice nap?" Sandra said as she leaned over to give Matt a kiss.

Larry leaned down and hugged the boy, and Jimmy watched his stoic father turn away so Matt wouldn't see the tears in his granddad's eyes.

"Your dad's going to step out and call Grandma Ginger and Grandpa Chris, and we'll be here to keep you company until he gets back."

"Yeah," Larry said, "Let's see if there's a ball game on TV."

"I'm also going to call Hollywood's Kennel to see if they can keep Patches for the next few days. Would you and Dad be able to drop her off this afternoon?"

"Of course," Sandra said. "I haven't talked to Hollywood in years."

Jimmy didn't want to leave the room and go downstairs. He wanted to stay right beside his son. He walked to the end of the corridor, stood by the windows overlooking a large greenspace, and punched in his in-laws' number.

"Ginger, this is James."

"Oh, hello, dear. How have you been? We haven't seen you in a while. Chris and I were just saying the other day that we need to have Matt over to swim before the weather turns cold."

"That's why I'm calling. It's about Matt. He's in the hospital."

"Oh, no! That's simply terrible. Was he involved in an accident? Is he all right?" Ginger always sounded like a newscaster on the local channel with her polished upper-crust manner of speech. It made Jimmy want to grind his teeth.

"He's been sick for the last few weeks, and the doctor has ordered some tests. They suspect something is wrong with his liver, and they will do a liver biopsy tomorrow morning."

"Oh, good heavens. That poor child. Chris and I are involved with the mayor's charity event this week, or we'd come right over. But you must call us immediately when you get any news."

Matt struggled to keep a civil tone. "Of course, Ginger, you'll be the first call I make."

∼

SANDRA HELPED Patches out of the backseat of her car, and the dog pranced happily up the driveway of the white wooden frame home. Hollywood looked much the same as she had when Jimmy was friends with Hollywood's son, Shane, while they were in high school and early college. Now both women had a few more wrinkles. Hollywood's hair was a little grayer, but she still wore bright, colorful clothes and oversized hoop earrings. On her wrists were enough silver bangles to make a belly dancer proud.

"Well, Sandra Ross, how many years has it been?"

"Too many, my friend."

"I remember us sitting on those hard benches in those baseball stands every weekend for what seemed like forever. You only had two young'uns to watch, but Bob and I had five, as you recall."

"I recall very well. They were all well-behaved good kids."

"Thank you for saying that. Come on in and bring that sweet Patches. What's going on with Matt?"

Sandra didn't know how much Jimmy wanted her to share, so she said, "He's been sick lately, and the doctors put him in the hospital to run some tests. He has to stay overnight, and, of course, Jimmy will stay with him. I wish I could keep Patches at my house, but I've got grouchy, spoiled old cats. I think Patches will be much happier here."

"Which hospital is he in? Shane's wife, Dena, is a pediatric nurse at So Cal's Children's Hospital."

"Yes, that's the one."

"I'll be sure to tell Dena to look in on Matt. She's a lovely woman and an excellent nurse."

"Thank you. I appreciate your boarding Patches on such short notice. I need to get back. It was great seeing you again."

∽

Angela kept looking at her phone, waiting for the anticipated phone call from Jimmy. He hadn't called or even texted, and now it was late afternoon. Maybe he was waiting for her to call him. After all, this wasn't the olden days. Women could phone men if they chose.

But that wasn't Angela. She was a modern woman, but not modern enough to embarrass herself if Jimmy was planning to ghost her. Had he taken what he wanted and walked away? Was she lacking somehow? Surely he would be man enough to tell her he wasn't interested in pursuing a relationship. Wouldn't he? How could she have been so wrong?

All these questions drove her crazy as she picked up her bag and headed for her car. Being around pets always made her happy and could lift her out of any funk. She was certainly in a funk.

∽

When Angela knocked on her door, Hollywood was drinking a big glass of tea in her living room. "Hey, sweetie," she said. "This isn't your day to check on my guests. What's the matter?" A thin, long-legged old greyhound was spread across her couch and wagged its bony tail when Angela walked in.

"Nothing really, I'm just at loose ends, so I thought I'd

check in on the dogs. They always make me smile. I see you've brought Gracie inside."

"She was so depressed out there in the kennel and missing her mom and pop. I thought a little time with me might cheer her up. She's an old lady and deserves to be pampered. Thankfully for her, she'll be going home tomorrow."

"You're the best, Hollywood," Angela said, kissing her on the cheek.

"I am, aren't I?" She laughed loudly.

"I'm going to check on the beasties. Any problems I need to know about?"

"No, thankfully, everyone looks good."

Angela walked through the kennel observing the animals Hollywood was boarding. The kennel was clean and smelled of the same germicidal deodorant and disinfectant used at the clinic. Some dogs slept in comfy beds, while others played in the exercise yard. She stopped when she saw a long-haired black dog with white spots. "Patches? What are you doing here?"

At the sound of her name, the dog's tail started wagging like a metronome. Angela smiled and reached out to pet her before jogging back to the house and into the living room. "Is that Patches or her twin sister?"

"Oh, yeah, Sandra Ross brought her by earlier to board her for a few days. Matt's in the hospital. Jimmy is with him and couldn't leave the dog at home."

"Matt? What happened?" Her voice was troubled.

"I'm not sure. She said they were running tests, and Jimmy was staying at the hospital."

Angela flushed with shame from all the negative thoughts that had formed in her mind earlier. No wonder Jimmy hadn't called her. Something was wrong with his son.

CHAPTER 16

Jimmy sat on the couch that folded down into a bed on which he'd attempted to sleep the night before. He'd tossed and turned while thinking about every possible outcome of the biopsy. Thankfully, Matt had dosed off while watching an action movie and was still sleeping as the first rays of the sun were showing through the blinds on the window.

The door opened, and a nurse dressed in pale blue scrubs rolled a cart into the room. "Morning," she said. "I hate to wake Matt up, but I need to check his vitals and replace the saline drip. They'll come in about fifteen minutes to take him down for his biopsy."

When Matt opened his eyes, Jimmy was beside him with a comforting hand on his arm. "Morning," Matt mumbled.

"Good morning, Matt. I'm your nurse today," the cheerful young woman said. "I need to check your blood pressure and switch out your saline bag. Then I'll give you a little something to help you relax."

"How long will I have this thing stuck in my hand?" Matt

touched an IV needle and plastic tubing that was taped securely to the top of his hand and connected to the IV bag.

"I'm not sure what the doctor's plans are, but she'll be here in a few minutes, and you can ask her any questions you have."

Jimmy thanked the nurse and touched the scruff on his face and neck. He needed to shave and brush his teeth. He yawned, rubbed his eyes, and sat beside Matt, hoping to keep him calm by talking about inconsequential things. It wasn't long before whatever the nurse put in the IV took effect, and Matt's eyes fluttered and closed.

Fifteen minutes later, Doctor Heller entered the room, followed by three other people wearing blue scrubs. She explained the procedure and how long it would take to Jimmy as Matt slept on. The doctor explained they would return Matt to this room after the biopsy.

After the orderlies pushed the bed down the hall, Jimmy looked around the empty room, sank into a chair, and reached for his phone. He punched in Angela's number and heard the phone ring several times before her voicemail picked up. Of course, he thought, she was working today.

He spoke into the phone and tried to sound better than he felt. "Hi, Angela. It's Jimmy. I'm sorry I haven't called sooner. Matt's here in Children's Hospital, and they're doing a biopsy on his liver." He wished he could tell her he was scared witless and felt like beating his head against the wall, but he didn't want to worry her. Instead, he said, "I just wanted to tell you what was happening. You can give me a call if you like."

When the door opened, he looked up, and his mother appeared wearing a small backpack and carrying two large paper cups. "Please tell me you brought a toothbrush and a razor," he said.

"I did, and I also brought you a cup of coffee. I know

you're not usually a coffee drinker, but I thought you could use the jolt this morning." She handed him the cup, and a warm smile crossed her face as she unzipped the backpack and pulled out the items she brought, along with a white paper sack. "And I stopped at the bakery to get muffins."

"How did I win the lottery on great mothers?" He put down the coffee and gave her a warm, heartfelt hug.

"Remember those thoughts when I'm nagging you about something, James Ross. How's Matt doing? I bet he's scared."

"Actually, he was pretty calm. They gave him something before they took him to surgery, and he was lights out."

"Your father has this big project at a construction site, but he's coming by at lunchtime to check on Matt. Do you know how long he'll have to stay?"

"No, the doctor said it depends on how he's feeling and if there are any complications."

"Well, it's a good time for you to take a shower, since I brought you a change of clothes. You do look a little rough this morning. It's been a long twenty-four hours for you."

You don't know the half of it, he thought. He'd spent much of the night before last in bed with Angela and hadn't slept more than three or four hours when he got home. There had been no time to shower yesterday morning, and he had not put on clean clothes in his rush to get to Matt. He could still smell her scent as he pulled his T-shirt over his head. Had she heard his message? Was she upset that he hadn't called earlier? He didn't want to admit his weakness, but he really needed her right now.

Unable to sit still, he paced back and forth in the hall. What was taking so long? It had been over three hours, and Matt still wasn't back. It was supposed to be a short procedure. Was something wrong?

The elevator doors opened, and his dad walked out dressed in his typical electrician's uniform: blue jeans, rubber-soled shoes, and a long sleeve shirt. "Jimmy, Mom says Matt's not out of surgery yet. Everything okay?"

"I don't know. We haven't heard anything." He rubbed his hand through his short hair and sighed. "I'm beginning to worry."

His dad squeezed his shoulder and followed him into Matt's room. A few minutes later, they heard the creaks and rattles of a hospital bed traveling down the hall, and the fear gripping Jimmy was replaced with relief when they rolled his sleeping son's bed into the room.

Doctor Heller was behind them, still in her surgical scrubs. "Mr. Ross, let's step out into the hall to talk for a moment."

"What happened?" Jimmy said as soon as they left the room. "What took so long?"

"There was a complication with some bleeding. Not usual, but still not uncommon. We kept Matt in recovery until his blood pressure returned to an acceptable range. Normally, I would release him to go home this afternoon, but I want to keep him overnight so we can monitor him."

"Is he in danger?"

"No, it's only a precaution, and we will closely monitor him. I've put a rush on the biopsy, and we will let you know as soon as the results are in." She patted him on the arm. "Don't worry, Mr. Ross, we'll take good care of Matt."

He returned to the room and saw anxious faces, so he plastered a smile on his. "Nothing to worry about. The doctor explained what took so long. There was some unexpected bleeding, and they kept him in recovery until everything returned to normal."

When he moved to the side of the bed, Matt opened his eyes and moaned. "It hurts," he said, reaching for the bandage on his side.

Jimmy pushed the nurse's button, and a few moments

later, a nurse came in to give Matt something for the pain. She had him take several deep breaths, and after a while Matt began resting comfortably again, so his father went back to work. After checking to be sure Jimmy didn't need her, Sandra left to go home, hoping to avoid the afternoon traffic.

The sun was setting as late September afternoon shadows crept into the room. The nurse appeared every thirty minutes to take Matt's vitals, and the boy would stir and talk for a while before falling back asleep. The nurse assured Jimmy that it was expected because of the drugs. She explained that after the pain medication was decreased tomorrow, Matt would be more alert and active.

Jimmy scrolled through his phone, reading about the day's events on his news and sports apps while trying to keep negative thoughts at bay. Even though he had left a message about Matt, Angela hadn't called or texted, which disappointed him and made him sad. How could he have been so wrong about her? She'd backed off at the first sign of a complication in their relationship.

The door opened, but expecting the nurse again, he didn't bother to look up.

"Jimmy," a familiar voice said. "I'm so sorry. I just got off work and didn't have a minute to spare with surgery after surgery, and I …."

Jimmy sprang up from his chair as Angela moved toward him and pulled her into his arms. He held her tightly, as if at any minute she might disappear. "You're here. Oh God, you're here. You'll never know how happy I am to see you and how much I need you."

And before she could say a word, he kissed her.

CHAPTER 17

Angela stepped back and touched her swollen lips. Jimmy's kiss left her weak in the knees and wanting more. But this was not the time or place, and his focus was on his son.

"Tell me what's going on with Matt. You must be scared to death." Jimmy's handsome face looked sunken and hollow, as if he had the weight of the world on his shoulders. She didn't know how to make things better for him. In his message, he said Matt was having a liver biopsy but nothing else. He told her to call if she wanted to. Of course, she did, but she also didn't want to intrude.

"Let's step out in the hall, and I'll tell you what I know, which, at this point, isn't much." He placed his hand on her lower back and guided her out the door, and she felt a guilty thrill at his touch.

"Matt's really sick, and I'm terrified of what the doctor will tell me about the biopsy results. I should have sought help sooner."

"He's young, Jimmy. You had no reason to think his upset stomach was anything serious, and besides, you did take him to the doctor. You said they did blood work." She touched his face and said, "You can't blame yourself."

"The doctor described a litany of things it could be. A viral infection, overuse of certain drugs, metabolic disorder, or cancer. All of them scary."

Angela knew from her medical background that Jimmy was right to be frightened and concerned, but she would remain upbeat for his sake and his son's. "Is there anything I can do for the two of you? Bring you anything?"

"No, I'm good on that end. My mom brought me a change of clothes, and she spent most of the day with us and stayed with Matt when I went down to the cafeteria to get something to eat. But I haven't had much of an appetite. I'm so happy you're here. It means everything to me."

They returned to the room and spoke softly until she heard Matt's high-octave voice say, "Hi, Angela. When did you get here?"

"A little while ago. I had to work, or I would have come sooner." She walked over to him, touched his arm, and said, "How ya feeling?"

"Yucky, but better than before. Dad says they put good juice in my IV."

Angela flashed Jimmy a grin and said, "He did, did he?"

Jimmy raised an eyebrow to give her a *who me* look. Angela was in so far over her head with this man and falling hard for him and his son. As she looked at the small boy in the bed, a sad, unsettling feeling settled on her. Matt was such a beautiful boy, with his dark hair and chocolate eyes. Jimmy was a lucky man to have this boy as his son.

She leaned over the bed and gently ruffled his hair. "If you're still here tomorrow, I'll check on you again after work. Anything you want me to bring you?"

"Patches," he said with a shy smile. "But I don't think they let dogs in here."

"I saw Patches yesterday. She was a happy girl playing with all her friends at Hollywood's Kennel. How about I check on her again tomorrow? I'll even take a video so you can see that she's doing okay, even if she misses you."

"Thanks, Angela. You're the best."

"So are you, kid. So are you."

∽

THE FOLLOWING DAY, Sandra breezed in with a big smile. Jimmy knew his mother's stomach was tied in knots, but Matt would never know it. In his eyes was the grandmother who cuddled him and loved him unconditionally. The grandmother who had stepped in after his mother died to comfort a heartbroken boy.

Jimmy hugged her warmly. "I love you, Mom," he said.

"Well, Son, I love you too," she said, looking perplexed.

"I don't say that nearly enough, and I just wanted you to know how much I appreciate everything you do, even if I sometimes take it for granted that you'll always be here."

"I don't have one foot in the grave yet, buster. I expect to be around a little while longer."

"That's not what I meant, and you know it. The same goes for Dad. I don't know what I'd do without you."

Matt was sitting in a chair while eating a breakfast of oatmeal with blueberries. The doctor had stopped all pain medication, and although he looked tired, some of his energy was coming back. "Hey, Grandma, they let me eat today. The oatmeal is yucky, but the blueberries are okay, and Angela sent a video to Dad's phone of Patches having fun."

"That was nice of her."

"She works at Hollywood's sometimes and checks up on the dogs boarded there. Did you know she knew Hollywood when she was my age? She used to volunteer there. I think that would be fun."

"That sounds like a fine idea. Maybe your dad can talk to Hollywood, and you could volunteer for a few hours over the Christmas holidays while you're out of school." She looked at Jimmy as if expecting a comment.

"Angela stopped by last night when she got off work to check on Matt," he said.

"She's a very nice young woman, and it's thoughtful for her to think of you both. I enjoyed our outing at the ballgame. I forgot to ask how it went when you two went out to dinner?"

Jimmy's eyes darted away from his mother and back to Matt as if what happened between them was written all over his face. "I had a nice time," he tried to say without smiling. A very nice time, he thought.

The door opened, and Dr. Heller came into the room accompanied by a young man. "Good morning, all," the doctor said. She introduced her companion as another doctor doing a clinical rotation since So Cal was a teaching hospital.

"Can you hop up here on the bed so I can take a look? How's your pain level this morning?"

"It doesn't hurt like yesterday unless you do that," he yelped as she removed the bandage and checked the incision spot.

"How's the nausea? I see you managed to keep the oatmeal down."

"Probably because I was starving. Oatmeal's not my favorite, but this morning it looked fantastic."

Dr. Heller smiled and gave him a soft pat on the shoulder. She shined a penlight in his eyes, listened to his heart and lungs, and then proclaimed, "The incision is healing as expected, and your vital signs are good. I'm sending you home this afternoon, Matt, with some restrictions. You will be on a special diet. No fast food or junk, like potato chips."

She looked at Jimmy and said, "And, Mr. Ross, no canned vegetables, hotdogs, or sausage. We are trying to limit the salt and fat intake. The nurse will give you a list of good and bad foods along with the discharge papers." She turned and spoke directly to Matt. "It's very important that you take the diet seriously, Matt."

"Yes, ma'am."

She helped him back down and into the chair to finish his breakfast. "Stay home and be lazy for a couple of days, and then you can go back to school and resume your normal exercise. I will call in a couple of prescriptions, too."

Jimmy looked at his mother and saw relief on her face, but he was waiting for the other shoe to drop. This was too easy. "What about the biopsy? Do you have the results?"

"Yes, I was getting to that. I need to have a conversation with you and your wife. I will get some background information and discuss some things."

"Matt's mother is deceased. It's only me."

"Oh, I'm sorry. I have an office in the hospital and will finish my rounds by eleven. Please stop by about eleven-fifteen. First floor, room one fourteen. Will that work for you?"

It will have to, he thought. I'd rather know right this minute than wait. Fear knotted inside him, but his voice was calm. "Yes, my mother will be here with Matt. Eleven fifteen is good." Whatever the doctor planned to say was not something she wanted to share with Matt, and Jimmy could feel in his bones it wasn't something he wanted to hear.

CHAPTER 18

"Come in, Mr. Ross," Dr. Heller said. Her office space was neat and sparsely decorated. No artwork hung on the eggshell white walls, only framed diplomas. "I recognized you immediately yesterday and wanted to say my husband and I have enjoyed watching you play baseball throughout your career."

"Thank you," Jimmy said, feeling a little embarrassed. This lady was a highly accomplished professional who saved people's lives daily. He had played a kid's game for a living.

Dr. Heller took off her glasses, wiped them with a cloth, and then replaced them on her long slender nose. "That being said, now let's talk about Matt."

"It's serious, isn't it?"

"I'm afraid so. Matt has a progressive liver disease. His liver is slowly being replaced by scar tissue. I have started him on medication to slow the progression of the disease and relieve some of the symptoms, but I'm sorry to say there is no cure." Her voice was soft, and he supposed she was trying to be comforting, but she was telling him his son would die.

Jimmy was speechless and could not form a coherent thought, much less speak. He put his head in his hands and tried to control his erratic breathing. Breathe in; breathe out, he chanted in his head.

"Mr. Ross, it's not hopeless. A liver transplant is an option. The success rate in adolescents is over eighty percent, and the long-term survival rate is excellent."

He opened his mouth to speak, closed it, and opened it again. Gulping for air like a fish out of water, he finally said, "Why, why Matt? What happened? What did we do wrong?"

"You did nothing wrong. Sometimes there isn't a clearcut etiology. For the next thirty minutes, she explained the reasons in medical terminology while showing him images of the liver. It could have been a virus, or it could be genetic. I can refer you for genetic testing if you're planning on having more children. It could also have come from his mother. Is there any history of liver disease in your family?"

"No, and it's impossible that it's from me or my late wife, Cindy. I'm Matt's father, but I'm not his biological father, and Cindy wasn't his biological mother. We adopted Matt when he was two days old."

To her credit, the doctor said nothing. She only steepled her fingers and looked at him with compassionate eyes.

"It was a closed adoption, and I don't know who his biological parents are. Is that something that you need to know? A lawyer arranged the adoption, so I could try to find out."

"It wouldn't have any effect on the treatment, but we'd have a better chance of getting a match if you could find the biological parents. Of course, we'll test you and your family and put Matt's name on the national transplant waiting list."

"Wait, I'm confused. Aren't transplants, except kidneys, since we have two, taken from people who are brain dead?"

"The liver is an amazing organ, Mr. Ross. It's the only one

that can regenerate and grow. We can take a portion of a liver from a donor and transplant it into your son, and within six months, the donor's liver would have grown back, and your son's would have reached normal size."

"What steps can I take to become a donor?"

"First, you'd need a compatible blood type with your son." She opened a screen on her computer and hit several keys. "I see Matt's blood type is B positive. That's one of the rare ones. Do you know your blood type, Mr. Ross?"

"Yes, I've given blood before. It's A positive." A knife sliced through his heart as he said the words.

"That's not ideal, but with treatments to lower your antibody levels, not impossible, but you wouldn't be our first choice. If we find a donor with a matching blood type, we test to determine HLA or human leukocyte antigen. That's a marker on your cells to tell which cells in your body belong and those that don't."

She gave him a warm smile and said, "I know all of this sounds technical and overwhelming. We don't have to discuss it right this minute. As I said, we will put Matt on medication, which will slow the progress of the damage, but barring a miracle, a transplant, will be in Matt's future."

"If that becomes necessary, will you do the surgery?"

"No, I will be his doctor, but a transplant surgeon with a trained team would do that."

She stood and said, "This is a lot to take in. Talk with your family, and we can make an appointment later this week for you to bring in Matt. He needs to understand what is happening and what he will face. He seems like a very intelligent young man and needs to be told as soon as possible."

After leaving the doctor's office, Jimmy felt like a zombie as he walked down the hall toward the bank of elevators, oblivious to everyone around him. It took him a minute until he realized someone was calling his name.

"Jimmy," Angela called out as she saw him walking toward her, but it was as if he didn't see her. She stopped right in front of him, and he would have walked into her if she hadn't put her arm out. "Jimmy," she said again. "Are you all right? Did something happen to Matt?"

"Angela?" he said, and suddenly she was in his arms. "Can we go outside? I need to get out of here."

She took his hand, and they walked out through the large glass doors toward several benches under large palm trees. It was windy, and her long hair whipped around her face. She sat and pulled Jimmy down to sit with her. "Tell me," she said softly.

He looked down at her hand and then up into her eyes. "What are you doing here? I thought you had to work today."

"I do. I took a long lunch to come to check on Matt. I called the room, and your mom said he wouldn't be released until this afternoon, and you were talking to the doctor. I take it things didn't go well."

Jimmy's face was solemn as he gazed into the distance, probably trying to stave off tears. She looked away, giving him time to get himself together as she rummaged in her bag, pretending to look for something.

Finally, he said, "The doctor says Matt will die if he doesn't get a liver transplant."

Angela bit back tears as she pictured the precious little boy's face. She could not fall apart. She needed to be strong for Jimmy, so she waited patiently for him to continue.

"Doctor Heller is putting him on a special diet. No fats or excess salt. She's also prescribing some medication to help slow the progression of the liver disease, but he will need a transplant soon."

He rubbed his eyes and said, "Did you know they can take a liver from a living person? Well, not the whole liver, but a portion of it." He raked his fingers through his hair. "Of course, you know all that. Listen to me; I'm babbling."

She squeezed his arm and said, "It will be okay. Living-donor transplants are highly successful now. As his father, if your blood type is a match, then your tissue typing will probably be a match as well. They will conduct an HLA test to be sure."

He squeezed her hand and turned to look at her. "It's not a secret, so I never think about it or have any reason to mention it. Matt's my son in every way that counts."

"Well sure, he is."

"But Cindy and I adopted him. We aren't his biological parents."

CHAPTER 19

Jimmy squeezed Angela's hand and looked into her kind brown eyes. "Thank you for coming. You're like a breath of sunshine on an otherwise crappy day. I don't even have the same blood type as Matt, which makes it nearly impossible for me to be a donor. I feel so useless not being able to do a thing to make him better."

Angela smiled softly. "You're his father, and he loves you. Being there for him is one of the most important things you can do."

With a long, exhausted sigh, he stood up. "Getting involved with me wasn't exactly what you were looking for, was it? I have a lot of baggage."

"Stop being so hard on yourself, Jimmy. Everyone has baggage and some more than others. You're not going to scare me off because things suddenly became complicated. I'll get tested as soon as Matt's doctor sets everything up. I'm a universal blood donor, so maybe my tissue type will be a match, too."

"I couldn't ask you to do that. It would upend your entire life."

"You're not asking. I'm offering. Besides, you upended my entire life the moment you stood across my exam table with water dripping off your face while holding a muddy, wet dog."

"The feeling is mutual, Angela Michaels. You're one of the most giving people I've ever met, and Matt adores you."

"He's a beautiful boy, and it's impossible not to love him. Let me at least see if I'm compatible. Then we'll go from there, okay?"

Overcome with emotion, Jimmy brought her to him in a fierce hug. While trying to swallow the tears threatening to fall, he answered, "Okay, I can do that. And never let him hear you call him a beautiful boy. It will completely blow his image."

Her gentle laugh broke the somber mood. "I've got to get back. If you get to take Matt home today, I'll stop by after work, pick up Patches at Hollywood's, and bring her to you. May I tell her what's going on with Matt? I'm sure she'll ask."

Jimmy moved back but kept his hands on her shoulders while giving her a serious look. "Of course. It's not as if we can keep it a secret, nor do I want to. Matt will need a donor, and I need to get the word out."

She kissed him softly and said, "I'll see you tonight. Text me your address."

∽

WHEN JIMMY OPENED the door to Matt's room, he heard the boy's infectious giggles and saw a petite brown-haired woman dressed in scrubs talking with his son. A different nurse than earlier, he thought. His mother who was sitting in a chair beside the bed was laughing, too.

"Dad," Matt said, "this is Dena Madden. She's Hollywood's daughter-in-law." He let out another giggle before saying, "She told me about how her dog ate their whole dinner when it was on the kitchen counter. And it was steaks."

"Hello," Jimmy said as the pretty woman who was several months pregnant turned and smiled at him. "You're Jimmy." She held out her hand as she said, "I'm Shane's wife. He told me stories about you two when you were in high school. Such a pleasure to finally meet you."

"Hollywood told me he was married to a pediatric nurse. It's nice to meet you too. Are you Matt's nurse this afternoon?"

"No, I'm up on the surgical floor, but Hollywood called to tell me your son was here, and I wanted to come down and say hello. I understand you'll be going home today."

He looked into her intelligent hazel eyes and could almost read the unspoken words. *But you'll be back soon.* He was sure she knew Matt's situation. He cleared his throat and said, "How's Shane? Until I talked to Hollywood a few weeks ago, I didn't know he was back from Colorado, much less married."

"He is fantastic and doing what he loves. He opened a clinic a couple of years ago with a fellow doctor he worked with in Colorado. Listen," she said softly, "If you need to talk." She looked at Matt, then back at Jimmy, and said, "If you need to ask about anything, please call Shane. Call even if you don't have questions. We'd love to have you and Matt over for a visit."

"Thank you, Dena. I appreciate that."

"I mean it, Jimmy. Because of HIPPA and all that, I don't know Matt's diagnosis. But from what Hollywood and your mother have said, I can guess what's happening. You're heading into murky waters, and Shane and I want to be there for you."

She gently squeezed his arm and said goodbye to Matt

and the others. Jimmy smiled as he watched his old friend's pretty wife walk out the door and back to work.

∼

ANGELA SAT in a wing-backed chair in Hollywood Madden's living room while sipping from a cold glass of iced tea. It felt good to get off her feet for a while, and the comfortable chair and colorful sofas made it a relaxing place. Hollywood's upholstered furniture had shades of purple and teal combined in various patterns. Somehow, the color scheme worked and fit Hollywood's vivacious personality.

After Angela confided in her, Hollywood became emotional. She had a big heart as well as a big personality. "Oh, that poor boy," Hollywood said as her eyes filled with tears. "And poor Jimmy. He must be beside himself with worry." Sorrow etched her face as she rubbed her arms, her bracelets clinking in the silent room. "Does Matt know how seriously ill he is?"

"No, not yet. Jimmy's taking him to see the doctor later this week so she can explain everything to him. He'll be on medication to make him feel better, but it's only a Band-Aid. He's going to need a transplant."

Hollywood's tone turned serious. "You're getting too close to Matt, aren't you, hon?"

Angela bit her lip and softly said, "Yes. It's impossible not to. He's such a sweet kid. And I really like Jimmy. He's the first man since Dean that I've cared about. His parents are wonderful, too."

"Are you going to tell him about what happened? I mean with you."

Angela never spoke about her past, not even with Hollywood, one of the few people who knew the complete story. "Not now. Someday, sure. I told Jimmy I would get tested to see if I was a transplant match. I need to do that," she insisted.

"It would surprise me if you didn't." She reached out and took Angela's hand. "You know I love you. I think of you as one of my kids. You let me know what I can do to help."

"You're sweet to ask, but I'm fine. Right now, I need to get Patches and take her home to Matt."

∾

THE DOG PRANCED with joy when let out of the kennel and rewarded Angela with a sloppy kiss when she bent down to secure the leash. "You're such a pretty girl. Now let's go cheer up your best friend."

Angela followed Jimmy's directions to a gorgeous beige colonial brick home with a manicured lawn and three-car garage. She parked her Honda on the street to avoid an oil leak from her old clunker on the smoky gray brick driveway.

She'd never thought about how much money Jimmy had, but now it was staring her in the face. The man was loaded. She shook her head. Of course, he was. As a star baseball player, he most likely had a lucrative contract plus endorsements.

She turned to speak to the dog, who sat patiently in the back seat. "I'm pretty sure I don't belong here, Patches. I'm just a girl from the other side of the tracks."

CHAPTER 20

When Jimmy opened the front door, Angela followed him into the spacious great room with gleaming white porcelain tile floors. Beside the sofa were a set of chic, modern armchairs, upholstered in a complementary fabric and positioned around a stylish coffee table "Wow," she said, "impressive."

"Hello and welcome. Thanks for bringing Patches." He leaned in and kissed her softly on the lips. "Pretentious, isn't it? Like something out of a magazine," he said, gesturing at the room. "Come to think of it, it was in a magazine." He laughed, and when he took the dog's leash, his hand brushed hers.

"It's a beautiful room. Don't you like it?"

"Not really, but it made Cindy happy. I'm more comfortable in the den. Easy chair, big screen TV. You know, guy stuff."

She gave him a quizzical look and shook her head, "Uh, not really, since I'm not a guy and haven't ever lived with one. But I'll take your word for it."

"You're kidding. You've never lived with a guy?"

"Nope, never. Where's Matt?"

"He's probably camped out in my chair. A couple of his friends from school came over to hang out with him. I didn't think it would hurt and hoped it would cheer him up. I've emptied all the cabinets and the refrigerator of anything on the doctor's list to avoid."

Jimmy motioned for her to follow and said, "Come on. Let's take Patches to him, and you can say hello."

Matt was sprawled in his father's comfortable chair. He wore shorts and a T-shirt and seemed to be all arms, legs, hands, and feet. He had the typical body of a growing boy nearing puberty. Angela refused to believe his life would be cut short and he would never reach his potential. She would do everything she could to see that didn't happen.

"Hi, Matt," she said. "I brought you a present." Patches wiggled and whined excitedly, her tail wagging as she put her nose against Matt's hand.

Matt moved and winced from the biopsy wound but flashed a huge grin. "Patches!" he said. "Hey, guys, Patches is home. Meet my friend, Dr. Michaels. She took care of Patches when Dad ran over her."

"Ouch," Jimmy said. "That's harsh. In my defense, it was dark, raining hard, and she ran out in front of my car."

Matt's grin had turned mischievous, and Angela suspected he was teasing his dad. A promising sign he was feeling better.

"It's okay, Dad. She still loves you." Matt rubbed Patches' head, then told her to sit and lie down. The dog obeyed the commands instantly, and Angela was impressed.

"Hi, guys," she said. "It's nice to meet you. Do you go to school with Matt?"

A kid with shaggy brown hair, big blue eyes, and a generous sprinkling of freckles dotting his face said, "Yeah, me and my brother live a couple of blocks down the street."

Jimmy looked at his watch and then at Matt. "You guys going to stay for dinner?"

"No sir, my mom will have a cow if we're late. Will you be at school tomorrow?" Both boys looked at Matt.

"I don't know. Will I, Dad?"

"As long as you feel good and take it easy, sure. I'll talk to the school nurse about giving you your medication."

∾

MATT WENT to bed after dinner, and Jimmy and Angela sat out on the back porch by the swimming pool. Since there was a chill in the air, he took a blanket and covered them both while pulling her close to snuggle.

Angela marveled at Jimmy's beautiful backyard, tall palm trees, ornamental shrubs, and various flowering plants. Soft ambient lighting was placed strategically throughout the backyard, creating an atmosphere that offered a serene retreat for relaxation and entertaining.

The focal point was the generous-sized pool, a shimmering oasis of crystal-clear water surrounded by flagstone tiles. The loungers were cushioned with weather-resistant fabrics in elegant patterns, and Angela thought it would be the perfect place to sunbathe or read. Completing the backyard was a well-equipped outdoor kitchen.

"Your yard is magical, Jimmy. Was this Cindy's design?"

"No, this is all mine. I'm happiest when I'm outside." He hugged her tightly and tilted her face up for a kiss.

"What if Matt wakes up and comes out?"

"What if he does? We aren't doing anything even if I'd like to," he said teasingly while rubbing her arms with his big hands. "Thank you for staying for dinner, such as it was."

"You're a great cook."

"Baked chicken and microwaved frozen vegetables don't

take a lot of skill, but the diet the doctor gave me doesn't leave room for much creativity. I have boxes of forbidden food to take to a local food pantry in the garage. The strict diet will to be hard to enforce."

"Yeah, he's almost a teenager, and I hear junk food is what they mostly live on."

"Does that mean you weren't ever a teenager? Did you just skip right to adulthood?"

If you only knew, she thought as she tried to relax in his brawny arms. She laughed and said, "No, but I'm a girl."

"You most certainly are," he said, kissing her neck. "While I was in Matt's room at the hospital today, I met Dena Madden, Hollywood's daughter-in-law. She is Shane's wife. Do you know her?"

"No, we've never met, but I've met Shane and run into him a few times. He left for Colorado right after med school, and I was in school myself, so we didn't cross paths very often. I take it you guys were good friends."

"Yeah, he's a great guy. We played baseball together in the summers when I was in high school, but baseball wasn't Shane's whole life like it was mine. He knew from the get-go that he wanted to be a doctor. Like you knew you wanted to be a vet, I guess."

"The idea always seemed out of reach, but, to my mother's horror, I was good at math and science. She thought girls weren't supposed to be good at those subjects. I graduated from high school a year early, and my guidance counselor helped me apply for scholarships. Because my grades were excellent and my socioeconomic level wasn't, there were several to choose from."

"How old were you when you went to college?"

"Seventeen."

"You were just a baby. Was it hard?"

"No, I loved school and not living at home with my

mother. She tried the best she could, I guess, but she was one of those women who wasn't cut out to be a mother. Matt is fortunate to have been adopted by you. Sometimes birth parents aren't the best people to raise a child."

"After Cindy and I got married, she wanted to wait a while to have kids and concentrate on her career. We were both twenty-four and thought we had lots of time. Then, when we decided we were ready, she couldn't get pregnant. We tried everything, and I told her no more after the fourth round of in vitro. It was tearing our marriage apart,"

"I'm so sorry," Angela said as she stroked his arm, encouraging him to continue.

"We fought constantly, and she complained because I was always gone. How could we have a marriage, much less a baby? I tried to convince her to come with me sometimes, and she did for a while, but she didn't like all the traveling, and you know the rest. Maybe that was the handwriting on the wall that ended with her affair later. I don't know."

Angela shivered, and he pulled her onto his lap, tucking the blanket tightly around her. "We chose to adopt a child, and one day she came home with the news that she'd found one. A young pregnant teenager didn't want to keep her baby."

"Then you know who Matt's birth mother is. That's good. Maybe she'll be a match."

"No, Cindy didn't know the name. It was handled by another lawyer. The mother wanted to remain anonymous. Something about her being famous, and we would have recognized her name. I don't know the details, but the whole thing was hush-hush. It's hard for me to understand how anyone could give up their own child, but I'm grateful every day, and we were so happy to get Matt."

She was sitting in his lap now and felt his magnetic pull, but this wasn't the time, not with the news about Matt, and it certainly wasn't the place. She sighed, leaned back, and closed her eyes but couldn't relax.

"Do you want kids someday, Angela? I couldn't help but notice how good you are with Matt."

She didn't know what to say or even how she should answer that question. It would open a conversation she wasn't willing to have. She slowly eased herself off his lap and stumbled over her words. "Yes, of course, but it's getting late, and I really should go."

"What's the matter? Did I say something wrong?"

"No, nothing. I'm tired, that's all. We both are. It's been a really long day. When do you plan to talk to the doctor again?"

"We have an appointment Thursday for her to explain everything to Matt. It's not a visit I'm looking forward to. I don't know how he will react."

"I think he will surprise you. I suspect he's a pretty strong kid. Will you ask the doctor when I can be evaluated as a donor and call me to say how everything went?"

"Sure," he said, but his eyes were questioning as if waiting for an explanation for her puzzling behavior.

She stood, folded the blanket, and then gave him a soft kiss on the lips. She would have to tell him soon, but not yet, because something he said tonight made her fear he would not understand.

CHAPTER 21

Jimmy watched Angela drive away until the taillights on her little Honda were no longer in sight. What had he said to upset her? The question about children? But she said she wanted them, so why did it bother her? Even though she denied it, he knew she was upset.

It couldn't be anything about Matt. She adored him. For her, it wasn't an act like it was with a couple of women he'd dated. He could tell the difference. What wasn't Angela telling him? Would Hollywood know? Would she tell him if she did? Probably not.

What did he know about Angela anyway? She'd grown up here in San Diego and was raised by her grandmother until she was fourteen and then by a single mother until she left for college. She'd been in love with a boy that died in a car accident. That's all he really knew. All she let him know.

Angela Michaels was an enigma; every time he was with her, he got to chip away a little more of the facade. Tonight, he'd learned she was a math and science nerd and left home for college when she was seventeen. He wanted to know more.

She never talked about friends, but everyone loved her at the emergency clinic, and of course, there was Hollywood. She'd dated that jerk. What was his name? Greg something. Had she slept with him? Did she compare Jimmy to him?

Maybe it was all his imagination. He tried not to compare Cindy and Angela. They were two completely different women from entirely different worlds. Cindy had been the proverbial spoiled rich girl with doting parents. She liked and wanted nice things. Thankfully, Jimmy had hit the majors early in his career and could afford the lifestyle she wanted. That they both wanted if he was honest with himself, or at least he'd thought so at the time.

He'd loved Cindy, but things weren't perfect before she died. Would they have stayed together? He didn't know. Probably if for no other reason than for Matt's sake.

Angela was the opposite of Cindy. Acquiring material possessions didn't seem important to her. Not as much as helping people did. She offered not to charge him for performing the surgery on Patches because she wanted to help a hurt animal and a distressed boy.

Whatever he'd said to upset her, he planned on making it right. No way was he letting Angela slip away without a fight. Was he falling in love with her? Yes, he thought. How could he not?

He heard a moan from Matt's room and Patches' soft whine. He rushed down the hall and pushed open the door to see his son sitting up in bed, his eyes wide with fright.

"Hey buddy, are you hurting? Did you have a bad dream?" Jimmy sat on the edge of the twin bed with its Spiderman comforter and pulled Matt close to him in a fierce hug. Soon Spiderman would give way to more grown-up décor, but Jimmy wasn't ready for that yet.

"I think I had a bad dream, and my side hurts a little." Matt hugged Patches as the dog slathered her wet tongue over his face.

"Dad?"

"Yeah."

"Thanks for letting me keep Patches. I love her a lot."

The room was dark, with only the light from the hall illuminating the bed, keeping Matt from seeing the tears flooding Jimmy's eyes. "I like her a little bit, too. She kinda grows on you, huh?"

"You're a big softy, Dad. I love you a lot, too." He ran his hand over Patches' silky ears, and then his voice became anxious. "Am I going to die?"

The question slammed Jimmy in the gut, and he grasped for the best words to say. Oh, God, please help me, he thought, his throat tight as he tried to answer. "No, you're not. Something is wrong with your liver, but the doctors will fix you up. We have an appointment the day after tomorrow to talk to Dr. Heller, and she's going to explain to us what she wants to do. She's looking at all those tests you took and the biopsy results. She's a good doctor, Matt. I looked her up, and she's top-notch."

"Am I going to have surgery?"

"Yes, but I don't know how soon that will happen."

"Will I still be able to play baseball?"

Jimmy hesitated and decided to think positive. "I'm sure you will in time, but that's one of the questions we can ask her. Why don't we think of all the other things we want to know and write them down?"

"Okay, let's do that. I like Dr. Michaels," he said. "Too bad she's not a people doctor."

"I'm glad she's a vet, because she got Patches all better," Jimmy said.

Matt lay back down, his head pressing into the pillow as

Patches circled twice and snuggled beside him. "Is she your girlfriend? Cause it's okay if she is. A couple of guys' dads at school have girlfriends, but they're divorced. And the guys think Angela's smokin' hot."

"They told you that?"

"Oh yeah, before they left tonight."

"She is pretty smokin', but let's keep that between us, okay? I don't know if she's my girlfriend or not. We haven't talked about it. But I like her, and she likes me. And even more important, she likes you, and you like her. But remember, you will always come first."

Matt yawned as his eyelids fluttered closed. "I'm okay, Dad. Don't worry about me. I can't even remember what I dreamed about now, and my side doesn't hurt anymore."

"You want to come sleep with me in case you wake up again?"

"Nah, me and Patches are okay here, but leave the door open, okay?"

"You bet."

Jimmy left the hall light on as he walked into the den and collapsed in his easy chair. His body shook, and muffled, soul-wrenching sobs escaped his throat as he hung his head and pulled at his hair. Salty tears rolled down his cheeks as a sudden rage twisted his emotions into a silent scream. He wanted to slam his fist through the wall as he gulped for air and felt an overwhelming sense of helplessness and grief.

His brave little boy. His baby wanted to know if he was going to die. And God help him, Jimmy didn't know the answer.

CHAPTER 22

Angela's phone binged with a text.

> Hi, Matt's appointment tomorrow is at eight-thirty. How about going to the beach with us after? You have a way of cheering him up.

> Love to. Pick me up at my house? What time?

> Don't know how long the doc will take. Let's go with 10:30 unless you hear from me.

She texted back a happy face emoji and smiled as she put her phone in her pocket.

Rachel, the all-around Girl Friday receptionist, clucked and said, "Don't you look happy? Got a date with Mr. Cutie?"

Angela lifted her eyebrows and said, "Who are you talking about?"

"James Ross, silly. You guys are dating, aren't you?"

Angela thought for a moment and realized that, yes, she guessed they were. "Where did you hear that?"

In a sing-song voice, Rachel said, "It's common knowledge. Everybody knows."

"Yes," Angela said, pushing open the door to the lab, "we are." She felt like she used to in high school, although the only boy she had ever dated back then was Dean, and she never invited the few girlfriends she had to her house.

She considered herself friendly but guarded and was trying to let more people in, but it wasn't easy. Any relationships she'd had in the past were superficial, like the one with Greg.

"Wahoo," Rachel pumped her arm up and down. "He seems like a really nice guy, and he's easy on the eyes."

"Yes, he's both of those things," Angela said, while suppressing a smile.

They both heard a ding signaling the front door opening and Rachel rushed out as Angela prepared for another emergency. The owner of a muscular Rottweiler suspected the animal had eaten something poisonous. Angela induced vomiting, administered medication to reduce the symptoms, and placed the big dog on an IV to flush out all the toxins from his system. They would hydrate him, keep him overnight, and probably send him home the next day.

Angela pushed her hair back and sat down at her computer to log into the dog's chart. When her phone buzzed with a text again, her heart skipped a beat when she read the message from Jimmy.

> Can you take a break?

> Yes, for about fifteen minutes. Why?

> Meet me in the parking lot, and you'll see.

As she closed the file and removed her stained lab coat, her stomach tied itself in knots. Had something bad happened? Stopping to tell Rachel she was taking a quick fifteen-minute break, Angela opened the front door and saw Jimmy standing by his car.

She was instantly relieved when she saw his entire face break out in a warm smile. It couldn't be anything serious if he was smiling.

"I brought you something," he said, reaching into the front seat.

Oh, please don't let it be flowers, she thought and laughed when he brought out a paper coffee cup and a white sack with a logo she recognized from a bakery down the street.

"I thought about you all morning, and I imagine you're tired after being up so late last night. I'm here to officially apologize for whatever I did to make you leave in such a hurry."

He leaned down and, oblivious to the people coming and going, kissed her right there in the parking lot. She could imagine Rachel gawking out the window. "Thank you. You're the sweetest man."

"I was going for sexy, but I guess sweet will do. I'm on my way to meet with my buddy Shane, Hollywood's son. He wanted to show me the clinic and catch up." He kissed her again, avoiding the sack and coffee cup, and said, "Are we okay?"

"Yes, we are okay, and you didn't do or say anything wrong last night. I was tired, that's all. I'm looking forward to tomorrow."

∼

JIMMY THOUGHT Shane Madden looked much the same except his blond hair was a little shorter now, and a few fine lines were etched around his smiling eyes. They shook hands as Shane said, "Great to see you. My wife and I took in a couple of your games since I've been back home. Congratulations on your retirement. You got to live out your dream. That's awesome."

"So did you," Jimmy said. "You're the doctor you always wanted to be." Jimmy expected to see a hotshot surgeon since that had been Shane's master plan.

"I can practically read your mind, old friend. I was living the dream in Colorado, or what I thought was the dream as an ER doc and surgeon while dating the boss's beautiful daughter. But what a person wishes for isn't always what they really want or need."

His arm spread out in a sweeping gesture as he said, "This is what makes me happy. I'm working with everyday people who deserve the same health care as the rich and famous. And I'm married to the love of my life. I'm a lucky man. Come on! I'll show you around and introduce you to my partner, Patrick."

After the tour, they sat in Shane's office and discussed playing baseball during their high school days, old friends still living in the area, and some crazy things they used to do. Jimmy patiently waited for Shane to bring up the elephant in the room.

Shane finally said, "You're a good friend to me, and I would have contacted you anyway when I found out you were back. But when my mother told Dena and me about your son, I wanted to reach out right away. I hope you don't mind."

"Of course not. I feel like I'm walking through a minefield. I've spent countless hours on the internet even though the doctors told me not to, but I need to know as much as possible about what Matt is up against."

"I will not presume to know as much as your hepatologist about liver disease, but I can tell you that the profession is making tremendous strides in treatments. Have they recommended a transplant?"

"Yes, the doctor will talk to us tomorrow and explain the process to Matt. He's a great kid and he's taking this scary situation extremely well. I don't know if I could be as composed as he is. What are we up against, really?"

"The success rate for liver transplants is very high, but there are some things to be concerned about. The biggest is rejection, and there is also the risk of infection and graft failure, but your doctor will explain everything. These complications are the exception, not the rule."

"Thanks, Shane, I appreciate the information. Like I said, I've been all over the internet, and it's pretty scary."

"You've met my wife, Dena. She works on the surgical floor at Children's Hospital, so you'll see plenty of her after the surgery, and she can run interference for you. Hospitals have a lot of rules and red tape."

"I appreciate that. By the way, congratulations on your baby."

"Yeah, we're excited. I was sorry to hear about your wife's death. I imagine it was challenging to raise Matt while continuing to play professional baseball."

"It was tough for a while, but I had a lot of help from my folks, and I'm so lucky that Matt's a good kid."

His thoughts drifted as he thought about how good his life had become after meeting Angela on that rainy night, and how happy he had been until Matt got sick. He wondered if his luck had run out. Now he was on a rollercoaster with no way off.

CHAPTER 23

Angela scooted out of Jimmy's SUV in the public beach parking lot about twenty miles up the coast from home. Because it was outside the San Diego city limits, dogs on a leash were welcome twenty-four hours a day.

Matt clipped a leash on Patches, and the three of them made their way down the winding path along the bluffs to the crescent-shaped sandy beach below. Angela could smell the coconut sunscreen they had rubbed into their skin and breathed in the salty scents of the sea.

Jimmy slung the strap of a cooler across his shoulder and reached for Angela's hand. Delighted that he was holding her hand in public, she looked up at him with a questioning smile.

"I have it on good authority that you are my girlfriend," he said with a grin. "That makes it okay to hold hands."

Her heart tugged, and her face shone with pleasure. It was a lovely fall morning on the beach with a soft breeze blowing, and for a moment, it felt like all was right with the world. "Matt said that?"

"Yeah, he did. He wanted you to perform the surgery, but he decided you couldn't since you're a vet."

She laughed and squeezed Jimmy's hand. When they reached the sandy beach, Jimmy set down the cooler containing icy cold bottles of water and Matt's approved snacks. He was sticking to Matt's strict medical diet.

Angela was eager to learn how the doctor's appointment had gone earlier that morning but decided not to bring it up. She thought it might upset Matt and ruin his day. The boy was unusually quiet, and that worried her.

"Do you think I can run a little?" He looked at both Angela and Jimmy.

"I think you will be fine," Jimmy said. "I've done a little research. But don't get waist-high in the surf. Save that for next time."

After they spread out thick towels and arranged the beach bags, Angela leaned down to pet the big dog. "I bet Patches would love to get her feet in the water. Most dogs can't resist getting wet."

Matt and Patches took off for the water while Jimmy set up a beach umbrella. Angela and Jimmy had settled onto the beach towels on the warm sand when Matt and a wet dog descended upon them. Matt grinned down at them. "Come on, guys. Go in the water." He tugged at Angela's hand to pull her up, and she did the same to Jimmy.

Angela felt self-conscious because she had not worn a bathing suit in public for years. Today, she wore an oversized shirt over her one-piece. Jimmy had no such qualms and slipped his T-shirt off in seconds, giving Angela an excellent view of his pecs and abs that she had intimate knowledge of from the night they'd made love. Looking at him made her feel all gooey inside.

"You're next," he grinned at her.

The Frisbee came out, and Patches gleefully chased it back and forth for what seemed like hours before they frolicked in the water and laughed like kids. Angela noticed Matt was struggling, and it was obvious he was getting tired. Jimmy thought so too, and she heard him say, "Let's take a break."

When they returned to the towels, Angela pulled water bottles from the cooler and handed Matt a small bag of salt-free peanuts. She had not found a moment alone with Jimmy to ask how Matt had handled the visit to the doctor. Perhaps it had gone well since Matt didn't appear traumatized.

Surprisingly, it was Matt who brought it up. "I saw the doctor this morning," he said, plopping down on a towel with Patches behind him. "The one that took a sample of my liver."

"Oh, and how did that go?"

"Not so good. I need an operation, but I already knew that 'cause Dad told me. The doctor said I need a new liver. Mine isn't working so good anymore."

Angela wasn't sure what to say, and saying I'm sorry didn't fit, so she waited for him to continue. She thought she saw fear in Jimmy's eyes along with a look of pride.

"I asked if I would still get to play baseball, and the doctor said I could, but not until I'm all healed up. That's the really bad part."

"You know what the good part will be?" Angela said. "You won't feel bad anymore. No more stomach aches or feeling pukey."

"Yeah, that will be good. The doctor explained exactly what they were going to do." He popped some peanuts in his mouth, chewed, swallowed, and then said, "Want to know?"

"Sure," Angela said, although she had already guessed most of it. For the next fifteen minutes, Matt explained his situation as only a twelve-year-old boy could do.

Angela was more determined than ever to get tested as a possible donor. She only hoped to be as brave as Matt, and she attributed a large part of his good attitude to the way his father was handling the situation. Although she knew Jimmy was a mess inside, on the outside, he remained the calm, caring father she'd always seen.

"I'm going in next week for a test to see if I am a match. If I am, I can donate part of my liver," Angela said.

"Wow, that's awesome. If you do that, then you'll be part of me."

Angela swallowed back tears at his sweet reaction. Recovering, she said, "Yeah, I guess that's what it means. I never thought of it that way." Fortunately, he didn't notice the tremor in her voice.

"Dad said he can't donate 'cause we don't have the same blood type. How come you can?"

"I'm a universal donor with type O blood."

"Lucky for me," Matt said and took a drink of water.

"It's not a sure thing yet, but yeah, lucky for both of us."

Matt looked up at Jimmy. "I'm tired. I think I want to go home now if that's okay."

"You bet." He pointed at the sleeping dog, "Look at Patches. She's all worn out too."

∽

WHEN SHE GOT HOME, Angela took a long hot shower to wash off the sticky sand from the beach. She was amazed and relieved at how well Matt had received the transplant news. When he had time to think about everything, he'd probably be more apprehensive, but for now, he was handling things much better than most adults would have.

After dressing in a pair of soft, worn jeans and a short sleeve blouse, she went outside to pull weeds and work in her flower garden. Her grandmother had taught her to garden, and she knew which plants would thrive in full sun and which would need more shade. Flowers bloomed in small colorful beds in her yard throughout the spring and summer.

Today, Angela dug up her iris plants, separated the rhizomes, and then replanted them to allow them space to bloom again in spring. She waved at her neighbor and gathered her gardening tools before going back inside, resigned to spend another night alone. This feeling was new. Before she'd met Jimmy, she had been content to go out to dinner occasionally or see a movie with Greg, but she mostly enjoyed her solitude.

When the doorbell rang, she peeked out the front window, deciding not to answer if it was a solicitor. When she saw Jimmy, she quickly swung open the door. "I wasn't expecting you. Is Matt okay?"

He stood there looking so handsome with his dark hair a little longer than when they'd first met as he smiled down at her. Before she could say anything more, he stepped forward, picked her up, and kissed her soundly on the lips as he kicked the door shut. "I've wanted to do that all day long."

His hands traveled down her back to her hips, pulling her against him where she could feel his erection. Breathing hard, he kissed her again as her lips parted for his tongue to mate with hers.

"You are driving me crazy, and I can't keep my hands off you. Do you know how hard it was to see your tight little body in that bathing suit all afternoon?" His hands moved toward her breasts, and her nipples hardened when he touched her.

She struggled to keep a rational thought and finally said, "What about Matt? Where is he?"

"Spending the night with his best buds. And yes, I gave all the necessary instructions to the kid's mother."

She leaned into him, and his mouth covered hers hungrily. She felt him shiver as she murmured against his ear, "Please take me to bed. I don't think I can wait any longer."

CHAPTER 24

Jimmy, relaxed and content for the first time in days, lay beside Angela, whose soft breathing revealed she was sleeping. Her long dark hair brushed against his chest as he watched her sleep, much like an angel for whom she was named.

He knew this peaceful feeling wouldn't last, but for a small measure of time here with Angela, he could have thoughts about something other than his precious little boy's illness.

As he watched her, he felt that tug he hadn't felt since the early days of his relationship with Cindy. He had been only twenty-one when he'd met and fallen in love with the pretty blonde rich girl. Just an inexperienced kid with raging hormones.

This time, he had years behind him, and he was falling hard for this woman. He knew there was something special about her from the very beginning.

She stirred, her soulful green eyes opened, and her gaze pulled him in. "Hi," she said, her voice husky from sleep as

ANGEL'S HEART

she reached up and touched his cheek. "I didn't mean to fall asleep. What time is it?"

"Not quite midnight. You haven't been sleeping for long." He kissed her fingers. "You are so beautiful," he said, and pulled her into his arms.

"I think you need glasses," she said, sounding playful.

"Nope. Last checkup, I was twenty-twenty." He pushed back the hair, partially covering her face, and said, "How'd you get your name?"

"From my grandmother. When she saw me sleeping in the hospital crib, she said I looked like an angel and convinced my mother to name me Angela. Mother wanted to name me Breeze. I think there's an air freshener out there with that name."

"Funny, that's exactly what I thought while I watched you sleeping."

"What? That I looked like an air freshener?" Her laugh was warm and sexy.

He kissed her then, taking care to go slow and enjoy the moment as he cupped her face and looked at those dangerous eyes he could get lost in. "I love you, Angela Michaels," he said and began to show her how much.

∽

ANGELA AWOKE EARLY and quietly eased out of bed. In the bathroom, she washed her face, brushed her teeth, and pulled her hair back into a ponytail. She'd never awakened in her bed beside a warm man before, not even Dean.

She wanted to stay right there and bask in the sheer pleasure of the night before, but she had too much to think about. Jimmy said he loved her, and she couldn't say it back. At least, not until he knew everything. But she had no doubts about being in love with him for so many reasons. He was a good man, a good son, and a wonderful father. He was also sexy, smart, and an exceptional lover.

She'd taken Dean's memory and tucked it safely away in her mind. Dean with his honorable, caring, and loyal moral code. She wondered how her life would have turned out if she'd never met him. She'd loved Dean with wild abandonment, as only immature love can be. But she was an adult now, and her feelings for Jimmy were solid and real. The two men were nothing alike, yet so similar in strength of character.

Angela slipped on her glasses to check the clock on the kitchen stove, which read five thirty-five. She was a morning person who liked to map out daily tasks early to see what lay ahead. Jimmy had to be home at seven when they dropped Matt off before his grandmother took him to school. She decided to make coffee before she woke him.

When she turned around, there he was, leaning against the door frame and giving her a lazy smile. He stood there in his denim jeans, riding low on his hips, barefoot, and shirtless. She gazed at the patch of hair that traveled down his chest and disappeared under his waistband. Her throat suddenly went dry as memories of the night they had spent together danced in her head.

"I was just coming to wake you up," she said. "What can I get you?"

"You, most definitely, but if that's not an option, then I guess a glass of water's fine." He walked toward her, kissed her softly on the lips, and took a seat at the small kitchen table.

She set the water in front of him and sat across from him with a mug of coffee. She slipped her finger into the handle of the mug, took a sip, and swallowed hard before saying, "We need to talk."

"Uh oh, that can't be good. Is this where you tell me you like me a lot, but...."

"No, that's not it at all. But you deserve to know about my past before we go any further. You told me you loved me. That's a big deal."

"What's so horrid about your past? From what I can see, you spent all of it in school or working."

She picked up her mug to take a sip of coffee and noticed her hand shaking. She used two hands to set it back down and said, "Do you remember at your house when you asked why I left so abruptly and what you had done wrong?"

"Of course, I remember. It was only a few nights ago. You said you were tired, but I didn't believe you. Still don't."

"I was tired, but that's not the reason I left. I wasn't upset with you. I was upset with my reaction to what you said."

He raked his fingers through his hair and asked, "Okay, what did I say?"

"You said you couldn't understand how anyone could give a child up for adoption." She put her hands around her coffee mug, and the words came tumbling out. "When I was sixteen, I got pregnant with Dean's baby, and he was killed before I even suspected." She stopped and took a ragged breath. "I didn't want to, but I had no choice. My baby was adopted. Please don't hate me."

She looked across the table at Jimmy, who was quiet for the longest time, his face expressionless. Finally, he said, "Why in the world would you think I would hate you? You were only sixteen, Angela, and probably scared to death. From what you've told me about your mother, I'm sure she had no plans of being there to support you."

"I wanted to keep the baby; believe me, I really did, but something went terribly wrong when I was in labor in the hospital. Doctors delivered a healthy baby, but I was diagnosed with a pulmonary embolism and lapsed into a coma for forty-eight hours. They didn't expect me to live."

Tears began sliding down her face as she said in a trembling voice, "When I woke up, my baby was gone. When I asked my mother what happened, she said she certainly was in no position to take care of an infant if something happened to me, so I had signed adoption papers. I can't remember much about the whole experience except for my pain and confusion. The family wanted a closed adoption, and I guess I agreed to it. I don't remember signing the papers. I don't remember much of anything about my hospital stay. By the time I recovered and could think clearly, it was too late. My baby would have bonded with the new parents already.

Her words came out in a rush as if she were cleansing her mind from her traumatic experience. She was fighting hard for control and choking back sobs.

Jimmy gently took both of her hands in his, and when she looked into his eyes, she saw no blame, no hate, not even disappointment. All she saw was love.

"I can say it now, Jimmy. I'm sorry I didn't tell you sooner. I love you too. How could I not?"

He stood, came around the table, and pulled her into his arms. "I know how hard it must have been for you to tell me that. Sweetheart, you have nothing to be sorry about. You had an impossible decision to make, and you made the best one possible due to the circumstances. Somewhere, there is a family who will be eternally grateful for the gift you gave them, just as I am, to Matt's birth mother. You're an unselfish woman with a tender heart, and I love you even more than ever."

CHAPTER 25

*A*ngela sat in the small room of the hospital lab, waiting to have her blood drawn to determine if she could be Matt's donor. This was only the first step in a tedious battery of tests, including X-rays, an EKG, and a CT scan. In addition, she would need to visit a psychologist and have a complete physical. She was eager to finish the tests and hopeful the results would be positive.

If so, those positive results would come with significant ramifications. If she had the surgery, it would require her to take a leave of absence from work and depending on someone to care for her while she was convalescing. Because nothing was certain, she pushed those thoughts away and would deal with them when she had to.

Her relationship with Jimmy was going nicely, even if a sleepover was seldom something they could do. Neither of them wanted to change anything about Matt's routine right now. The boy was okay with his dad having a girlfriend, and that's as much as he needed to know now.

Kathy had called earlier that morning, and having her mother both call and visit within the last few weeks was unusual. Kathy asked how Angela was doing, whom she was dating, and whether she had seen James Ross since the ball game. As usual, she offered unsolicited advice suggesting that dating a man with a son wasn't the best decision and said that Angela should hold out for someone who wasn't encumbered.

Kathy always had an angle, but Angela couldn't figure out what it was this time. Since when had she cared who Angela was dating? And how did she find out? It wasn't as if they ever had girl talk. Kathy had finally achieved the social status she'd always wanted. She had plenty of money and men to buy her things. What was going on with her? After twenty-nine years, could Angela dare to hope the woman wanted to mother her? No, although her mother loved her in her own warped way, she was up to something.

∽

ANGELA WAS EXHAUSTED when she got to Hollywood's Kennels, but she looked forward to seeing the dogs and having a quick visit with her friend. She hadn't talked to Hollywood since she'd told Jimmy about her pregnancy.

She noticed a small SUV parked in the driveway. Hollywood probably had company, so since this was purely a social visit, she'd just pop her head in to say hi, check on the dogs, and leave. She was surprised when a pretty woman who was several months pregnant answered the door. Angela immediately recognized her from her picture.

"You must be Shane's wife, Dena. I'm Angela Michaels, Hollywood's friend, and the veterinarian in charge of all the fur babies' health."

"Angela, how great to meet you! My mother-in-law has spoken about you so often that I feel like I know you. Come on in. Hollywood's in the kitchen, but she'll be right back."

"I can't stay. I was in the area and wanted to drop by and say hi."

Angela heard the tap of Hollywood's boots on the shiny tiled floor as her friend slipped into the room, the scent of her telltale signature carnation perfume wafting behind her. She carried a tray with two ice-filled glasses, a frosty pitcher, and a plate of cookies.

She broke into a friendly smile as she said, "Angela, what a delight. Did you meet our sweet Dena?"

"I did, and I'm so sorry to interrupt."

"You're not interrupting. Would you like a glass of lemonade?"

It looked good, and she had nothing to eat or drink all morning while undergoing the required tests. "Maybe I'll have some and stay for a little while, but I'll get myself a glass after I check on the dogs."

∽

WHEN SHE RETURNED, both women looked up, and she realized they'd been talking about her. It made her self-conscious as she sank into one of the comfortable chairs and said, "Did I miss something?"

"I was telling Dena that I've known you since you were a teenager and that you and Jimmy are seeing each other."

"Oh, do you know Jimmy?"

"I met him the other day at the hospital where I work. My husband and Jimmy are old friends, and since I'm a nurse, Shane asked me to look in on Matt and introduce myself. How is Matt doing?" she said, her voice was soft and caring.

"For a kid facing what he's facing, I'm astounded at how well he's doing," Angela said. "I know he must be scared, but he's such an amazing kid. He met with the hepatologist, and she explained the transplant procedure to him."

"Have they found a donor?"

"Neither Jimmy nor Matt's uncle has a compatible blood type, and the four grandparents' ages disqualify them." She sipped her lemonade and said, "My blood type is O which makes me compatible. I've spent most of the morning having tests done to see if I can be a donor."

"Angela, what a remarkable thing to do!" Hollywood said as her eyes misted with tears. "You've always been such a dear girl."

"Yes, I agree," Dena said. "Especially since you can't work for at least four to six weeks. I understand that you're a veterinarian. That's not a simple sit-in-a-chair in front of a computer job. I imagine it's quite physical."

"It can be yes. I'll cross that bridge when I have to. It might all be moot if one of the tests disqualifies me."

Dena reached across and squeezed Angela's hand. "You're a courageous woman, and I admire you. The procedure won't be easy on you, Angela."

"I'm sure you would do the same for someone you love." Angela's words hung in the air as she suddenly realized they were true. She loved Jimmy, and she also loved Matt as if he were her own. She had no choice but to give the boy the chance to live.

Dena finished her lemonade, looked at her watch, and slowly rose from the sofa. "I need to run. Shane and I are going crib shopping when he gets home."

"How exciting for you," Angela said. "Do you know if you're having a boy or a girl?"

"Not yet. We haven't decided if we want to know. What do you think, Hollywood?"

"I always thought the surprise was worth the wait, but nowadays, there are so many more clothes and so many fun things to buy for babies. I think I'll let you and Shane make up your own minds without any help from Grandma."

Dena hugged Hollywood and then turned to Angela. "I work on the surgical floor of Children's Hospital, so I'll be there when Matt has his transplant. I told Jimmy to let me know if he had any questions or concerns. Matt isn't my patient, so I don't have any medical knowledge about his case yet and couldn't talk about it if I did, but just so you know, I'll be there. If there's anything you need, just ask."

∾

AFTER DENA LEFT, Hollywood put down her drink and arched an inquisitive eyebrow. "Not that I'm unhappy to see you, but what are you doing here? You're not the type to come over and visit without offering to do something. What's going on in that pretty head of yours?"

"I thought we could talk for a minute. I told Jimmy about my pregnancy and about giving my baby away."

Hollywood gave her an encouraging look. "And how did that conversation go?"

"He was wonderful and said all the right things. He said he was in love with me, and I know I'm in love with him and his son. Do you think I'm projecting because Matt is the same age as my baby would be now?"

"I don't know. Are you?"

"No, I don't think so. I was shocked when Jimmy said he and Cindy adopted Matt. He told me that the birth mother was some famous person, so everything had to be hush-hush because she wanted a closed adoption. Did my mother ever tell you anything about my baby?"

Hollywood's jaw clenched, and her eyes narrowed. "Your mother wouldn't even let me in the hospital room after you got out of intensive care. What she did to you was criminal."

"I still remember nothing that happened. I was a minor and had no rights. It's much too late now to go looking for my child. Who knows, maybe someday he'll want to find me. I pray he doesn't think I gave him up because I didn't want him."

Hollywood moved beside Angela and pulled her into her arms as Angela's head rested on the kind woman's ample bosom. She held her there and stroked her hair, offering comfort and concern. "You're a darling girl. Anyone who meets you knows you're someone special, and they can't help but love you."

CHAPTER 26

Angela stood on Jimmy's doorstep with her finger on the doorbell as wind whipped her long hair across her face. The weather in the city was almost perfect except for the strong, ever-present Pacific Ocean breeze.

She had news about the tests and thought telling Matt and Jimmy in person would be better than calling.

"Hey," Jimmy said when he saw her. As he opened the door, his brows pulled together and the lines on his face tightened as he quickly said, "What's the matter? Is something wrong?"

"Nothing. I didn't mean to frighten you. I wanted to give you the good news in person. Is Matt around?"

"Yeah," he said, leaning in to give her a welcoming kiss. The tight lines on his face relaxed. "What's up? I thought you were working?"

"I left early because I got a call from the transplant team." Her eyes twinkled as she tried and failed to tamp down her excitement. "I'm cleared to be a donor for Matt. You should hear from them tomorrow."

Jimmy placed his big hands on her shoulders and pulled

her in for a fierce hug. "I can never repay you for this precious gift, and I don't know what to say except thank you, and I love you."

"How's the little guy doing today?"

"Not so great. Having a bit of a pity party. Upset and angry about baseball. He's scared but won't admit it, and to top it off, he's almost a teenager, so I'm sure hormones are involved."

"Let's go tell him now," Angela said. "Maybe the news will cheer him up." She heard a noise from the TV as they approached the den and was surprised to find the room empty. "Maybe he's taking a nap," she said. "I can wait until he wakes up."

"No, he shouldn't be sleeping now. Come on. If he is, we'll wake him up."

Jimmy knocked softly on the closed door and said, "Hey, Bud, wake up. Angela's here with some news." Hearing no response, he knocked harder and opened the door. The dog lay on the bed, but Matt wasn't in his bedroom.

Jimmy quickly checked the bathroom, and Angela followed him as he walked through the house, while calling Matt's name. Jimmy let Patches out to relieve herself while they checked the backyard and pool area.

"Maybe he went to a friend's house."

"Not at this time of day and not without telling me." Jimmy rubbed his hands across his face as his eyes widened with concern. "And why did he leave Patches here?"

Angela didn't know what to think. Her experience with twelve-year-old boys was nonexistent except for her time with Matt. She didn't know how his mind would work if he were angry or scared, but she knew how she had felt when she was young. "Would he have run away?"

"Where would he go? He's not that close with Cindy's parents, and if he'd gone to mine, Mom would have called me immediately." He pulled his phone out, and Angela listened as he contacted Matt's friends, but none had seen Matt. Two boys had talked to him on the phone earlier that morning.

"Okay, let's think," she said. "You said he was angry about baseball. What was he upset about?"

"That he can't play this spring. In the past, his whole life revolved around spring baseball. He said he'd forget everything if he couldn't practice."

"Maybe that was his way of feeling close to you when you were on the road. He would be doing the same things you did every day."

"I never thought about it that way." His eyebrows arched with a realization. "But I think I might know where he is." Jimmy grabbed his car keys from a hook by the door leading to the garage and said, "His bike's gone, and so is his bat. Come on, let's go."

Five minutes later, Jimmy parked in front of a building with a sign above large double doors that read *Batters Up Batting Cages.* "Do you think he actually rode all the way here?" Angela said as she looked around the parking lot, hoping to see him.

"I'm pretty sure since that's his bike chained up over there." Jimmy's eyes danced with relief as he squeezed her hand. "I think we've found him. Now, I'm not quite sure what to do with him. I want to hug him and yell at him all at the same time."

"Do you think I could talk to him before you do either one? Believe it or not, I think I can relate to the anxiety he might be feeling. Not about baseball, but I suspect it goes much deeper than that."

"Be my guest. It will give me time to get control of my temper and my heart rate." When they entered the facility, Jimmy pointed to where he thought Matt would be and then sat on one of the long benches.

Angela found Matt in moments and saw him standing inside a steel-framed cage surrounded by netting. It was a far cry from the flimsy cages she'd seen while watching Dean practice. She stood silently and watched Matt take his stance with feet apart, knees bent, and hands near his shoulder as he slammed each ball that sped toward him.

She moved close to the netting when the cycle he'd paid for ended. Hoping not to startle him, she called out his name softly. When he turned, a look of uncertainty crossed his face before he gave her a guilty smile. "I guess I'm in trouble, huh? How'd you know where I was?

"I don't know why you'd think you're in trouble," she said, sarcasm dripping. "Your dad figured out where you were."

"Is it because I left without telling Dad and rode my bike on a busy street?"

"Those seem like two good reasons for your dad to be upset. I mean, it was a pretty thoughtless and selfish thing to do. He was afraid something bad might have happened to you. Is it your dad's fault you're sick?"

"Course not. I just ..." He put his bat over his shoulder and walked out of the cage to where Angela stood. "Why are you here?"

"I came by your house tonight to tell you something important. But guess what? You weren't there."

"I'm sorry, okay? I'm a horrible kid." He kicked the metal pole with the toe of his shoe and crossed his arms as he sulked.

"I get it, Matt. I lived with my grandmother, and she died when I was about your age. I loved her more than anyone in the world, so I left my house and walked for miles, telling no one where I was going. But unlike you, I didn't have a father to come look for me, and my mother didn't even know I was gone. I went to a park and sat there for a long time. Until it got dark."

"And your mom never came to look for you?"

"No, we weren't close, and I don't think she knew how to be a mother. I was sitting there mad at the world until a nice boy named Dean came over to talk to me. He liked to play baseball, too, and he was there at an old batting cage that was nothing like this one. Dean sat down beside me and told me he didn't have a mother or a father, and at least I still had a mother. Maybe she didn't know how to show that she loved me, or maybe she was born broken, but it wasn't my fault."

"Is this some kind of story that is supposed to have some deep meaning and make me feel bad cause I was a jerk?" He sounded amused.

Angela ignored his comment and continued. "He also told me it was okay to be scared because things always change. He'd been in more foster homes than he could count. Some of the foster parents were good people, and some were bad. He said I needed to make the best of my situation."

"What were you scared of?"

"The future. Life without my grandmother, who raised me." Angela put her arm around him and pulled him close. "That day, I made a friend I could count on and felt better and stronger. You have so many wonderful people in your life who love you. Your father, your grandparents, your friends, and now you have me. You'll never be alone."

"I'm scared, Angela. For Dad's sake, I tried not to be, but what if I'll never be the same? What if my whole life changes and I won't be me anymore?"

"Ah, the great unknown," she said, holding him closer. Then she touched his heart and said, "You will still be the same Matt Ross in here. Besides, there's no reason to think that any of those bad things will happen. After you've had time to heal, you should be able to lead a normal life."

Matt sighed and looked at her with tears welling in his eyes. Angela took a deep breath and continued. "Today, I'm just as afraid of the unknown as you are, but I am also so happy and grateful. The doctor told me I was a match and could be an organ donor for you. They will transfer a piece of my liver to you, so you can get well. We will both have our surgeries at the same time, and that's as scary for me as it is for you. But we have each other and can be brave and strong together. It will all be worth it. I promise you that."

Matt leaned in and wrapped his arms around her as she held him close and stroked his thick, dark hair. He pressed his face into her shoulder and sobbed as the feelings of fear and sadness he'd tried so hard to hide overwhelmed him.

CHAPTER 27

Matt sat propped up on pillows in his hospital bed, surrounded by a room full of people. Jimmy sat silently while taking in the whole party atmosphere. The entire family was doing their best to keep Matt's spirits up the night before the transplant surgery.

Angela, whose hospital room was next door to Matt's, sat by his bed, listening to Matt crack corny jokes. His latest was, "Patches is a genius. I asked her what was two minus two, and she said nothing."

He got the expected groans and yucks. When he ran out of jokes, Angela began regaling the room with her exploits as an emergency vet.

"Tell Grandma about the cat you had to talk to," Matt said, grinning.

"Oh, that was a good one. A lady brought her cat Cheeto in and asked me to please tell the cat what I would do. Then she asked Cheeto if he agreed, and of course, he told her I was an excellent vet, and he trusted me." Angela looked up with laughter and held up three fingers as she said, "True story, I promise."

Ginger, who was Cindy's mother, stood up and moved closer to the bed, and spoke to Matt. "You looked tired, dear." Then her gaze fell on Angela. "I'm sure you have many more amazing stories, but don't you think Matt needs his rest? He has a dangerous surgery tomorrow."

Jimmy came out of his seat immediately and was beside Matt in two strides. What could his former mother-in-law have been thinking to say such a thing? Angela quickly enveloped Matt in her protective shield. "I'm so sorry, Ginger, but you are mistaken," Angela said.

Angela took Matt's hand and said, "Matt is young, not diabetic, and his kidneys are working fine. There is no reason to believe that his surgery is more dangerous than any other major surgery."

"James said you are a veterinarian. I doubt you are qualified as an expert on the human body, much less a liver transplant."

Angela's tone was measured and patient as if she were placating a child. "That's partially true, but I've done extensive research and talked to several specialists. I feel confident in what I'm saying. Does your research say something different?"

"Well, no ... I ..."

Ginger's husband, Chris, joined her at the bedside and touched her shoulder. "Matt, I'm afraid your Gigi has been watching too many medical shows on television. Everything is going to go fine," he said, bending over and giving him a hug. "You've got nothing to worry about. We'll see you tomorrow after you're out of surgery."

"Thanks, Grandpa," Matt said as his eyes swept the room.

Chris's eyes narrowed when he spoke to his wife in a commanding tone. "We're going home now." Then he turned to Angela and said, "It was nice to meet you, young lady, and thank you for what you're doing for the boy."

Jimmy nodded but did not speak to Ginger as the couple left. He was afraid of what he would say if he opened his mouth. Ginger had always acted like an elitist with a stick up her butt.

The room was enveloped in uncomfortable silence until Matt finally said, "I guess Gigi really stepped in it."

A burst of relieved laughter filled the room. Grandpa Larry slapped his knee. "I couldn't have said it better." Then he stood and said, "I'm gonna take a couple of laps around the floor up here. Why don't you join me, Angela? I bet you'd like to stretch your legs."

Angela squeezed Matt's hand and said, "Sure, I'd like that. I imagine a walk down the hall won't be quite as easy tomorrow."

"Don't you worry about it. I'll be here and take you for a spin."

Jimmy watched Angela leave the room, walking arm in arm with his father, and thought how perfectly she fit in with his family. She was warm and friendly as well as intelligent and witty besides being the most compassionate and generous person he'd ever met.

He didn't know if she'd told her mother about the surgery, but if she hadn't, it wouldn't be a secret much longer. His agent had called several times to tell him that rumors were circulating about Matt's health. It was only a matter of time before the reporters tracked him down and thrust all of them into the glare of a media frenzy.

∽

ANGELA AND LARRY strolled past the nurse's station when the older man said, "Are you scared, honey? Cause if you are, nobody would ever know it?"

"Yeah, a little, but like I told Ginger, I've done a lot of

research and talked to the doctors at length about what the surgery entails and what the recovery will be like. I think I'm ready."

"Ginger had no business trying to scare Matt like that. That woman can be downright mean at times. Jimmy's wife Cindy was a nice enough woman, but she had a lot of her mother in her. Spoiled is what I'd say she was. I'd appreciate it if you kept this conversation between the two of us. She was our daughter-in-law, but I don't think she ever approved of us.'

"But she loved Matt, didn't she?"

"That she did. Maybe to a fault, but that's neither here nor there now. Sandra and I didn't see as much of Matt as we'd have liked when Jimmy was on the road. Course, we made up for that in spades after Cindy died."

No one, including Jimmy, had said anything bad about Cindy, but Angela was beginning to see a picture of the woman that didn't put her in the best light. She didn't feel like she was competing with Cindy's memory. They were nothing alike from what she could gather.

Angela was as far from a wealthy socialite as she could possibly be. Anyway, a good memory of a person always shined brighter than it actually was. She should know since she'd placed Dean on a pedestal after his death. But he wasn't perfect. No one was.

"Matt is fortunate to have you and Sandra as grandparents. He loves you very much, and how you feel about him is obvious."

Larry stopped, placed his hands on Angela's shoulders, and turned her to face him. His voice was full of gravel and emotion. "My dear, if there is ever anything in this world that you need, you only need to ask. We are so grateful to you for saving Matt's life, and before you say that anyone would have done it, you know that's not true. It takes a special person to do what you're willing to do, and we love you for it."

Angela wiped her eyes where tears had gathered and thought this must be what it would be like to have a father who cared about her. How lucky Jimmy was to have grown up in their home.

"Jimmy and Matt are fortunate to have you. You're a very nice man, Larry." She patted his arm and said, "We better get back, or Matt will think I ran away, and the nurse will come looking for me since I'm not in my room."

As they made their way down the hall, she saw a welcome and familiar sight. Hollywood Madden was coming out of the elevator, and she had dressed up for the occasion. She wore a long denim skirt, a white flowing blouse, and her trademark turquoise squash blossom necklace. Her boots clacked on the hard white tile, and her signature smile was bright and cheery.

"Hello, darlin'," she said, engulfing Angela in a warm hug. "I couldn't get here sooner. Had to get everything all settled down at home."

She looked at Larry and smiled. "You've grown old, Lawrence, but then so have I. It's been years. Saw your pretty wife a few weeks back. Now she hasn't changed a bit."

"It's always a pleasure to see you, too, Hollywood. Jimmy tells me you knew our Angela when she was younger."

Angela's heart warmed when she heard Larry say 'our Angela' as if she belonged to their family. She hadn't felt she belonged anywhere since her grandmother died.

"I did indeed. She was always magical with my critters, a hard worker, and now she's my dear friend."

Angela's heart was overflowing because she knew that no matter what happened tomorrow, she would not be alone. She had Hollywood and Jimmy's parents who cared about her, and she had Jimmy and Matt. How different her life was now. How full and richly blessed.

After Hollywood and Matt's grandparents left, Angela said goodnight to Jimmy and Matt. She lay in her bed looking at the ceiling with her mind too full to fall asleep. She walked herself through the surgery and recovery period a million times. She wished Jimmy could be with her, but she knew he couldn't leave Matt alone. What if the sweet boy woke up and his dad wasn't there? She was a big girl, and she would be fine. Just like she told Matt, there was nothing to worry about.

She jumped when her phone buzzed and smiled when she saw Jimmy's name. "Hi, gorgeous. I took a chance you wouldn't be asleep."

"I'm trying, but …"

"Your mind is going in a million directions. I know. Mine too."

"How's Matt?"

"Finally went to sleep, but he's restless."

"And you? How are you?"

"Scared and feeling helpless. I love you, Angela. Tell me everything is going to be okay."

"Everything is going to be okay, and I love you too." Much later, Angela fell asleep with her cell phone still connected to Jimmy tucked against her ear.

CHAPTER 28

"When do you think they'll be here?" Matt said, his eyes bright and wide with curiosity and anxiety.

"The nurse said they'll be in a little before six to start you on fluids. That should be anytime now." Jimmy gazed out the window where the city below was still asleep with only a few headlights of early morning traffic. He'd showered, shaved, and packed his meager belongings in his backpack because Matt would not return to this room.

Jimmy heard a soft tap on the door as his mother poked her head in and said, "Morning, guys." Larry followed behind her with a smile on his face.

"Hi, Grandma, Grandpa," Matt said in a high-pitched voice. Jimmy watched his son rub his hands together and knew the boy was nervous.

To distract him, Jimmy suggested, "How about we go next door and tell Angela good morning. I imagine they'll take her to surgery first."

"Will you tie my stupid gown thing in back, Dad, so I don't show my butt to everybody?"

Glad that Matt still had a sense of humor, Jimmy smiled and said, "You betcha."

They could see Angela sitting on the edge of her bed in her room. She had already been connected to an IV bag, and she was visiting with Hollywood and Dena Madden. "Hi, guys," Angela said. Her voice sounded strong, with no sign of nervousness.

She motioned to Matt, and he crossed the room to stand beside her. She leaned close to him and whispered something in his ear. Matt hugged her tightly and said, "I promise."

Jimmy watched as they all hugged Angela one by one and assured her they'd be thinking about her. Jimmy was impatient to be alone with her before they wheeled her down the hall. He would never ask what secret she had told Matt. If either of them wanted him to know, they would tell him. But he wondered.

Hollywood stood and declared in that brisk, bright way she had of speaking, "I'm going down to the cafeteria to get coffee. If you'll show me where the surgical waiting room is, Dena, I'll meet everyone there." Before they left, she said, "Anyone else want something from downstairs?"

No one did, and Jimmy's parents took Matt back to his room next door. Finally, Jimmy had the precious private moment alone with Angela he'd wanted. He sat on be bed beside her and took her into his arms. "You're the bravest woman I know, and I love you so much. I'll be right here when this is all over. Do you want me to call your mother?"

"No, I told her I was having surgery today and why. She told me I was an idiot. She asked if she needed to come to the hospital or if I would need a ride. I told her that was all taken care of." She looked up at him with a serene expression in her eyes. "Don't feel sorry for me. I came to terms with my mother's lack of empathy a long time ago. Like I told Matt, I think Kathy must have been born broken."

He reached out and pushed back a lock of her hair that had fallen across her eyes. "I hope you know that now you have me and my family. We all love you."

"I know, and I'm so thankful." She put her hand on his face, and her eyes searched his. "Jimmy, everything is going to be fine. Matt will be fine, and so will I. Since this new procedure for living donor liver transplants uses laparoscopic surgery, I'll have a minimal scar and still be able to wear my bikini."

"I'm going to hold you to that since I've yet to see you in a bikini." He chuckled and teased her. "I doubt if you even own one."

"You'll see, mister." Her eyes danced with mischief, and although he knew she must be frightened, it was not in her nature to ever let it show. This kind and beautiful woman had a tough shell and a tender heart.

He leaned in to kiss her again when the door opened and the staff from her transplant team walked in.

∼

JIMMY LISTENED to the click-clack of knitting needles as his mother's hands crafted her latest project. It was a strangely calming sound that reminded him of his childhood when he used to sit in front of the television on Saturday nights. Four hours had crawled by, and he'd run out of conversation. He had no interest in reading today's newspaper or the book he'd picked up in the gift shop.

The comfortable waiting room had cushioned chairs and a large sofa. A Keurig-K commercial coffee machine sat on a long table with wicker baskets of individual coffee pods in different flavors, tea, and hot chocolate. A phone with a direct connection to the operator downstairs hung on the wall with a big screen television next to it. It was tuned to a game show with the audio muted. Jimmy was grateful for that. Having to listen to the sound of a laugh track while sitting in the surgical waiting room would have been torture.

Ginger had called earlier to say she and Chris had an appointment that morning, but they'd be up after lunch. She said he should call if anything came up in the meantime. Came up? Jimmy had given up years ago on his expectations for Ginger and Chris. Ginger was a cold, selfish, self-centered woman, and Chris, although pleasant enough, had absolutely no backbone.

Hollywood had gone home to check on things and should be back within the hour. Someone from the transplant teams for Angela and Matt had been in periodically to update everyone. Everything was going as expected. Whatever that meant, Jimmy thought. It had seemed like a damned open house.

He looked out the window, and Dena startled him when she touched him on the shoulder. "They're finishing up with Angela. There were no complications with the surgery, and she should move into ICU soon."

"And Matt?"

"Everything looks good so far, but his surgery is much more complicated than Angela's, so it will be a few more hours for him. You have time to get something to eat if you want."

"No, I'm not hungry, but thanks, Dena. I appreciate you doing this."

"It's my pleasure. I'll check back in with you in a little while."

The door opened again, and Hollywood bustled into the room, striding purposefully toward him. "What's the matter?" Jimmy asked as she reached him.

"There's a circus outside, and your mother-in-law is

getting her fifteen minutes of fame, along with Kathy, the witch."

"What are you talking about?"

Hollywood held up her phone and showed him the live-streaming news interview of Ginger talking to a local reporter about Matt's surgery. She was rambling on about how traumatizing it was for the entire family and that it would have upset her dear departed daughter Cindy to see her poor baby suffering.

Hollywood touched the screen of her phone and scrolled until she found another video of a pretty woman who resembled Angela who was saying how lucky she was to have raised such a special, giving daughter."

"I'm assuming that Kathy, the witch, is Angela's mother?"

"Yes, and she'll play it for all it's worth. She probably came upon Ginger being interviewed and pushed her way in front of the camera to get her share of the limelight."

Jimmy groaned and rubbed his eyes. "You said something about a circus outside."

"Channel 8 and Channel 10 news vans are parked out front. That reporter woman with the short curly hair from one of them is poking her microphone in everyone's face. It's good that this is a children's hospital, or she'd be up here demanding to talk to you. A person must have ID and parent or hospital permission to be anywhere on this floor."

"I guess the cat's out of the bag now, and I'm pretty sure how it got there."

"That would be my guess, too. Can't imagine why Ginger would want to exploit her grandson that way, but it takes all kinds."

The phone on the wall rang, and Larry got up to answer it. Cupping his hand over the receiver, he said, "There is some woman outside who says she's Angela's mother and wants to come in. What do you want me to tell security?"

Jimmy looked at Hollywood and watched her vehemently shake her head no.

"Tell her to come back tonight when Angela's awake," Jimmy said, hoping he was making the right decision. The woman had missed her chance to come before the surgery when it might have made a difference for Angela to know her mother cared. He wasn't a big enough person to sit in the same room and make polite conversation with a woman he didn't know but already despised.

CHAPTER 29

Angela's mind swirled with a sorrowful dream from which she couldn't awaken, try as she might. The kindest, dearest person she had ever known was gone forever. She couldn't stomach the condolences that neighborhood friends offered in hushed tones, along with casseroles and desserts. She knew these neighbors meant well, but the house full of mourners just made her feel worse. Especially since they were all speaking to her mother instead of to her. Didn't they know Kathy wasn't the one who would miss Angela's grandma? Kathy had never been there for her mother or daughter unless she needed something.

Angela let the screen door swing shut behind her and walked and walked until she could no longer hear the low buzz of sympathetic conversation surrounding her at her grandma's house. She wore her church dress and shoes as she walked past the row of houses and into the park. It was the first time she'd wandered so far from home alone.

Her friends at school thought Angela was sheltered, and maybe she was, but going to school and helping at the dog kennel on weekends made her life full. She planned to work at the kennel more often this summer because it would be lonely at Grandma's house.

She knew it wasn't her grandma's house anymore. Her mother had made that clear after the funeral when she said in front of all her grandmother's friends and neighbors, "This is my house now, Angela, and things are going to change around here. Your days of being spoiled are over."

Angela's eyes were swollen and puffy. She hadn't even tried to hold back the flood of tears that threatened to choke her since her grandma had closed her eyes and taken her last breath. The sun was low in the sky, and it would be dark soon, but no one at the house would care. She would bet her mother didn't even know she was gone. School was out for the summer, and Angela had nowhere to go and no idea what awaited her at home.

The few families at the park were packing up their soccer balls and leaving. Occasionally, someone would jog by on the walking path, but soon the grassy area would be deserted.

When she heard the whack of a baseball bat, she looked toward two old wire cages and saw a boy hitting balls. She chewed on her bottom lip, sat on a bench, and tried to make herself as invisible as possible in the shadows of the trees.

She closed her eyes for a second and heard a voice say, "You shouldn't be here. It's getting late."

She jerked her head up and saw the boy from the batting cages standing before her. When he removed his baseball cap and wiped his brow, his thick curly dark hair danced in the breeze, and his chocolate brown eyes smiled down at her. He was tall and every bit as good-looking as any movie star in the teen magazines she would glance through at the grocery store.

"What?" she said, trying to sound coherent. He had startled her, but she didn't fear him.

"It's not safe here after dark. You need to go home."

I wish I had one, she thought. Her grandmother's house wasn't really her home anymore. At least not like it was before. "I … uh… can't go home right now. My grandmother passed, and … well … it's complicated."

He leaned his bat against the bench and sat down beside her. "I'm Dean Scully. I haven't seen you here before."

"Angela Michaels, and I've never been here before."

"You don't go to the high school. I would remember if I'd seen you."

"Last year I went to a private Catholic school. I don't know what will happen this coming year."

"Private school? You rich?"

"No, I had a small scholarship, and my grandmother paid for the rest. It was something she wanted for me."

"Yeah, I plan on getting a college scholarship."

"For baseball?"

"Nah, it's fun, and I'm good at it, but I plan to depend on my grades and test scores to get me in. So, what's your story?"

"Story?" She looked down at her clothes and noticed one of her shoes was muddy.

"You said it was complicated and that your grandmother died. Is that why you're all dressed up?"

"Today was her funeral, and I had to get away from the house."

"I'm really sorry about your grandmother, Angela, but your parents will be worried about you. Come on. I'll walk you home."

Angela snorted and said, "I sincerely doubt that. I don't have a father, and my mother probably doesn't even know I'm gone. My grandmother raised me because my mother flitted in and out of my life. She would only come back whenever she was down on her luck. After my father dumped her and disappeared, she said she didn't have the time or patience to raise a daughter."

"She actually said that? To your face? You sound angry."

"Not really. I overheard her talking to Grandma a few years back. I'm used to how she is, but sometimes it hurts, you know?"

She saw the troubled look on Dean's face and said, "I'm sorry. You didn't sit here to hear me complain. You don't have to walk me home. I'll be fine, and I'm sure your folks will worry."

"I don't have parents anymore. I'm a foster kid. My mom and dad died when I was six. I've bounced from home to home ever since, but I finally got lucky. The family I'm with now are good people. At least you have a mother, even if she's not real good at her job." He gave her a crooked smile, pulled out his phone, and said, "I'll shoot my foster parents a text to let them know what I'm doing. No problem."

"I'm so sorry. You must miss your parents a lot."

"I can't remember much because I was so young. But I have some pictures, so that helps."

As they walked along, Angela felt bad because the walk was farther than a quick couple of blocks, but the time passed quickly because Dean kept the conversation flowing. He was different from most of the boys in her school. He talked about what he wanted to do with his life and how he loved animals and would be a veterinarian. By the time they reached her house, she had become infatuated with Dean Scully and didn't want the evening to end.

"This is where I live," she said, her throat tight with emotion. It was a small house in a working-class neighborhood that had always been her home. Her mother said there would be changes. She had no idea what that meant. Would Kathy sell the house and move away?

"Do you have a phone?" Dean said, surprising her. "I'd like to see you again."

"No, not a cell phone. Just a landline."

"Give me the number, and I'll call you."

She rattled off the number, and he entered it into his phone. "Smile," he said and snapped a picture. "I'm putting it into my contacts as Angela Michaels, the prettiest girl in San Diego. The girl I'm going to marry and spend the rest of my life with."

He hugged her gently, and she could smell his masculine scent of soap and sweat. She blushed and thought he might kiss her, which was crazy since they'd just met. Had they just met, or had she known him forever? She'd never kissed a boy, yet she knew she'd kissed this boy before. They'd held and touched each other and made love. Everything was moving so fast. It wasn't today anymore. She looked up at those eyes she could drown in. She'd seen those eyes before. But wait. He was walking away. Leaving. "Don't go. Please."

She moaned, knowing she needed to tell Dean not to leave. And what about the baby? And then she woke up.

∼

"You're dreaming, beautiful. I'm not going anywhere," Jimmy said, smiling down at her. "You had us a little worried with your Sleeping Beauty act." The doctor had assured him that, although not commonplace, some people experienced delayed emergence when under anesthesia. It had taken Angela longer than normal to wake up.

Her eyes widened in fright. "Matt?" she whispered in a raspy voice.

"He's still in surgery, but everything is going as planned."

She shook her head and said, "Matt," again, her voice edged with panic.

"Angela, it's Jimmy. I'm here with you. Matt is doing fine, and so are you. You came through like the champ I knew you'd be, and Dena is giving us frequent updates on Matt."

He looked at the nurse before leaning in to give Angela a gentle kiss on the forehead. "I can't stay but a minute, but I'll be back as soon as they let me."

Angela's eyes closed, and Jimmy just stood there looking at her until he heard the nurse clear her throat. "Sorry," he said, turning to the woman in the blue scrubs hovering near the bed. "She seemed so upset about my son, Matt. She's doing okay, isn't she?"

"Yes, all vital signs are good. Nothing to worry about. It's normal for a mother to worry about her son."

Jimmy didn't correct her and nodded as he left the ICU and returned to the surgical waiting room, where he was met with the anxious looks on his parents' and Hollywood's faces.

CHAPTER 30

Jimmy read a text on his phone and quickly made his way to the hallway near the elevators. He saw a shapely woman dressed in tight designer jeans and a sheer black blouse facing the uniformed security guard.

When she saw Jimmy, she said, "You must be James Ross. I've tried to convince this ogre to let me in." She pointed to the tall, muscular man with a shaved head.

Marcus was the private security guard Jimmy had asked his agent to hire after the news about Matt went viral that morning. The guard's instructions were to keep anyone not on the approved visitors' list away from the waiting room. "How did you get up here on this floor?" Jimmy said.

Jimmy immediately knew who she was. This woman hadn't seen sixteen in a couple of decades, but she rolled her eyes like a teenager. He patiently waited for an answer.

"I told them who I was at the desk downstairs and insisted they allow me to see my daughter."

"And who is your daughter?" Jimmy said, enjoying the moment way too much.

"Angela Michaels." She pulled her hair away from her face and tucked it behind her ears. "I've been here for hours and keep getting the runaround."

"Of course," Jimmy said. "I can see the resemblance. You're Kathy. I saw you on the news this morning."

"Katherine. My name is Katherine."

"A Kathy or Katherine isn't on the approved visitation list of family and friends. This is a children's hospital, and they can't let just anyone in to see a patient."

She huffed and sputtered. "I'm not just anyone. I'm Angela's mother." She looked around as if expecting an audience, and her voice softened as she said, "Is my daughter all right? She's had this terrible surgery, which is so brave of her, and you won't let me see her."

"It's not up to me, ma'am. She's in intensive care, and visitors are restricted. I'll ask her if she wants to see you now or wait until after they move her into a room."

"And when will that be?"

"Sometime tomorrow if everything continues to go well."

"Please tell my daughter I don't appreciate you keeping me from her, and I'll be back tomorrow to see her."

"This all could have been avoided if you'd told Angela you wanted to be here when she informed you about the surgery. You would have been on the list."

She made a rude sound, pivoted on her two-inch heels, and strode toward the elevator without looking back.

Jimmy shook his head and wondered how Angela could have become such a wonderful woman while having a mother like that. He turned to the guard and said, "Thank you."

"No problem, Mr. Ross. It's an honor."

ANGEL'S HEART

During his ten-minute visit, Jimmy stood by Angela's bed and cradled her hand. He looked up when the glass door slid open. Dena crossed the room, put her hand on his arm, and smiled. "It's all over, and Matt is doing great. They will wheel him into the ICU in a few minutes. You'll have to leave now, but as soon as they have Matt all set up, I'll come get you so you can see him. The doctor will come to the surgical waiting room to talk to you in a few minutes."

Jimmy squeezed the sleeping Angela's hand and leaned over to kiss her. "I'll be back, sweetheart. Matt will be here with you soon."

∾

The waiting room was empty. Jimmy had persuaded his parents to go home and said he'd call when the surgery was done. They wouldn't be able to see Matt today anyway, and Hollywood had to get back to work.

While he waited, he called Hollywood and both sets of grandparents, even though he was still fuming from the stunt that Ginger had pulled with the TV interview earlier that morning.

The lead surgeon from Matt's transplant team strode into the room, beaming. Jimmy had liked the doctor since they first met because of his easy-going personality and kindness to Matt. Plus, his friend Shane highly recommended and praised the man.

"Mr. Ross," he said and held out his hand. "Everything went exactly as planned. Not even a hiccup. Matt will be in intensive care for at least two days. He's on a ventilator now, and we will remove the breathing machine when the transplant team thinks best. It may be when he's ready to go to a room or even sooner."

Jimmy's hands shook, and tears sprang to his eyes as he took in the good news. "Thank you, Doctor, for everything."

The doctor put his hand on Jimmy's shoulder, acknowledging his thanks and his relief. "He'll be asleep when you see him. After you do, go home and get some sleep. There is nothing more you can do here tonight. He will be surrounded by a team of nurses. They have your number and will call you immediately if there is any change, but at this point, I don't expect that to happen. Your boy's a strong one. He is going to be just fine."

∼

WHEN JIMMY ENTERED THE ICU, he sucked in his breath as the nurse escorted him to where Matt lay sleeping. The ventilator mask took up half of Matt's pale face. He looked so small and vulnerable. Jimmy sucked in his breath and tried to steady his trembling hands.

Jimmy felt someone come up beside him and was relieved to see it was Dena. "I know it doesn't look that way, but he looks good. They'll take that nasty ventilator out tonight, and he'll look like himself again."

"I really appreciate you staying here all day for us. Shane's a lucky man."

"Thank you, but I'm the lucky one. I got both a wonderful man for a husband and a terrific mother-in-law. My own mother passed when I was a little girl. Shane said to tell you he'll swing by tomorrow."

"He doesn't have to do that. I know he's a busy doctor."

Her pretty eyes gave him an earnest look. "It's something he wants to do. You're his friend. I'm going home now, but these ladies and gentlemen in here are as good as it gets. They will take excellent care of both Matt and Angela. Go home and try to get a good night's sleep."

JIMMY STOPPED by Angela's bed and was pleased to see her eyes open. "Hey, you're awake."

"Sort of. I heard them bring Matt in. How's he doing?"

"Good. He's asleep and is still on the ventilator. It's scary, Angela. He looks so tiny."

She reached for his hand and said, "I know, but soon all this will be over, and he'll be on the road to recovery. We both will, and this will only be a memory. You're a good father, Jimmy."

He paused for a moment and then decided to be honest with her." Your mother was here."

"Oh, good Lord. Where is she?"

"I sent her home and told her to come back tomorrow. I'll tell you all about it in the morning."

"Okay, good."

She gave Jimmy a weak smile, and her eyes closed as he whispered, "I love you."

Jimmy found the security guard and sent him home for the night. "What time do you want me back in the morning?" Marcus said.

"I plan to be here at six," Jimmy said. "How about I meet you at the parking garage elevators, and we can walk in together? Hopefully, I'm old news to the press by now, but they could still be hanging around."

As JIMMY APPROACHED his SUV and clicked the key fob to disengage the locks and car alarm, from out of nowhere, the woman he'd seen interviewing Ginger on the morning news program stuck a microphone in his face while a cameraman shined a brilliant light in his eyes.

"James, it's Carolyn Dubois from Channel 8. Can you give us a minute of your time?" She leaned her back against the driver's door of his vehicle. He couldn't get in without physically moving her.

"I have no comment."

"But you don't even know what my question is. People are interested in you. You were a popular player in this city. Is it true your son is having a liver transplant, and your girlfriend is his donor?"

"I have no comment. Now, please get out of my way."

"Is it true that your son is adopted and …."

Jimmy's voice went cold. "Do not talk about my son." He reached into his pocket and took out his phone. "You have five seconds to leave, Carolyn from Channel 8, or I will call the police and press charges for harassment. You are obstructing me from entering my vehicle. Move now. One, two, three …"

"Fine," she said and moved the microphone away from his face before stepping out of his way. "Turn off the camera. I think we've got what we need."

Breathing deeply to steady himself, Jimmy slammed and locked the car doors. Then he considered what he'd told Marcus. Evidently, he wasn't old news after all.

CHAPTER 31

Jimmy arrived at the hospital early in the morning. He easily found a space close to the elevator in the parking garage and was glad to see the private security agent waiting for him.

"Good morning, Mr. Ross," Marcus said as he punched the elevator button for their floor.

Jimmy looked around but didn't see any news vans or reporters. "Morning. I had company when I got to my car last night. The gal from Channel 8 was waiting for me along with her cameraman."

Clearly upset, Marcus said, "I'm so sorry. I should have walked you to your car. That was my fault for not anticipating an ambush."

"Water under the bridge. She left after I threatened to call the police and file charges. We'll be better prepared tonight."

Once upstairs, Jimmy quickly made his way toward the nurses' station. He'd called early that morning to check on their condition, and both Matt and Angela were progressing well. As the doctor made rounds this morning, Angela would be moved to a room.

When the nurse escorted him to the ICU to visit Matt, Jimmy was ecstatic to see his son was off the ventilator. When Jimmy touched his hand, Matt mumbled a weak hello.

It hurt Jimmy to see all the tubes and wires sticking out of his son's body, but he was grateful the surgery had been successful without complications. Matt was in the first stages of recovery and hopefully everything would go smoothly. "Hey, buddy. You're looking good. How are you feeling?"

Matt licked his lips and said, "Thirsty."

One of the nurses put a straw to his lips. "Here you go. Take a small sip."

Matt's eyes, glazed with pain and medication, looked up at Jimmy and said, "Daddy, I'm okay. Don't worry."

Jimmy swallowed the hard lump in his throat and struggled to control his emotions. Matt hadn't called him Daddy since he was in kindergarten. "Okay, I won't."

"Angela's over there," Matt said, moving his head slightly to the right. "She's okay too. Like we promised."

Jimmy smiled, remembering the whispered words between them he could not hear the night before the surgery. "I love you, kiddo. I have to go now, but I'll be back in an hour." Matt's hand relaxed, and Jimmy knew he had fallen asleep.

He made a quick detour and found Angela awake, too. She looked much better than she had yesterday and gave him a sweet smile. "Did you get to see Matt?"

"I did, and he is looking as good as expected. A lot like you, with tubes and wires everywhere." He ran his fingers down her cheek and then caressed her face. "You look marvelous," he said in his best Billy Crystal voice.

"It's the new fashion. I'm leaving here this morning, and boy, that will be nice. Maybe they'll let Matt and me share a room. We can keep each other company."

He kissed her softly, this time on the lips. "I've gotta go before they throw me out."

∽

LATER THAT MORNING, after Angela had been wheeled into her room, she settled back in the hospital bed with her upper body slightly inclined and lay waiting for the shot of morphine to travel through her veins. Damn, but she hurt. Two nurses helped her take a few steps around the bed, and she felt like she was climbing a mountain with each step.

Jimmy and his parents had just left to see Matt. All three could visit him together if they didn't tire him. Angela's room was filled with beautiful bouquets of flowers. The emergency clinic had sent her stargazer lilies, along with a lovely note.

It floored her earlier when a volunteer delivered a potted plant with a card from Greg. Jimmy opened the card and frowned before he read it to her. "Even though we aren't together, I think of you fondly."

All she could think of was, wow. Did it make her a bad person to be secretly pleased that Jimmy was a tiny bit jealous? Especially since she wasn't the most beautiful creature now with her greasy hair and hospital pallor.

After her pain level eased, she drifted to sleep in her drug-induced haze. When she opened her eyes, Hollywood was there, and the room smelled of carnations. "Hi," Angela said. "When did you get here?"

"About five minutes ago. Jimmy said you were up and moving this morning."

"I guess I missed him. Poor guy, trying to be in two places at once. Yeah, they were torturing me and recommended an encore this afternoon. How's Patches doing without Matt?"

"She's a little lonely. Poor baby. I let her sneak in at night with me and my dogs."

"You're a softy, Hollywood Madden."

"Please, you'll ruin my reputation."

Angela's thoughts kept returning to the strange dream she'd had. Even though she couldn't recall most of it, she remembered Dean's eyes and how much they reminded her of Matt's. Brown was the most common eye color. Her eyes were brown. It was nothing. Even so, it nagged at her.

"Hollywood, I have a huge favor to ask of you, but if you don't have time, I'll understand."

"What is it, dear? I always have time for you."

"I have a photo album in a box on the top shelf of my closet. I need you to bring it to me. You still have my spare key."

"I can do that. Do you need it today?"

"No, whenever you have time. You can wait until I'm released from the hospital."

She patted Angela's hand and said, "I can probably get it done tomorrow."

"You're not going to ask me why I need it?"

"No, hon, that's none of my business."

Feeling the need to share her thoughts, she said, "I had this dream …." The door swung open, interrupting her words, and Angela's mother walked in. Kathy wore heavy makeup and was dressed for an evening out, not a hospital visit. Angela wondered what her mother was up to now.

"It's about time they let me in to see you. Whatever were you thinking keeping me off the visitors' list?" Her tone was somewhere between exasperation and anger.

Angela rubbed at her forehead, where an instant headache throbbed, and sighed. "Hello, Mother. I didn't keep you off the list. As I recall, you said you disapproved of the surgery, and you wouldn't be here."

"Well, I don't recall that's how the conversation went at all. You're my only child, and although I thought your actions were rash, I also thought them generous and selfless. I totally understood. You've always been such a good girl."

Angela fought hard to suppress a laugh, but it hurt too much. She was rewarded with a hateful stare from her mother. Wisely, Angela changed the subject. "You remember Hollywood Madden, don't you?"

Kathy looked at Hollywood as if the other woman were something she should scrape off her shoe. "I don't believe I do."

"I can't imagine you'd have forgotten me, Kathy. I sometimes picked up Angela and gave her a ride to my kennel when the weather was bad so she wouldn't have to ride her bike. You were always so kind." Sarcasm dripped from her tongue.

"Oh, of course, you're that Hollywood," she said.

Angela noticed she used the false, pretentious voice she sometimes affected to impress people. "Mother, how many people who live here in San Diego do you think are named Hollywood?"

"Well, I'm sure I don't know. A few, I imagine. But I do remember now. It was that horrible job you had working with dogs. You always came home stinking of them." She gave a derisive sniff. "And now you still do. Why couldn't you have been a real people doctor?"

Hollywood stood, her bracelets jangling, and kissed Angela on the cheek as she whispered, "Patience, dear. This too, shall pass. I need to go, but I'll see you sometime tomorrow."

Angela grimaced as she adjusted the bed to a more upright position and waited for Kathy to explain why she was there. She had no illusions it was only to visit, and it didn't take long.

"Darling, I suppose you haven't had a chance to see it, but I gave this marvelous interview about you on that morning show yesterday. And guess what? They want to interview both of us as soon as you're up to it."

"No." The word resounded in the air, and Kathy looked like she'd been slapped.

"What do you mean, no? You must do it, darling. It will be such fun."

"I'm not going on TV and pretending we are this great mother-daughter team when we're not. I will not lie and say you were supportive of my decision. You were not. I can't stop you from talking to the press, but I can refuse to take part in this ridiculous charade. I will not help you use Jimmy and his son for your own selfish purposes, whatever they are."

Angela gripped the sheet with her fists and pushed out the next few words through clenched teeth. "Only a few days ago, you were the one who warned me to stay away from Jimmy. Now, you want to pretend we're all best friends."

"What an ungrateful child you are. I did the best I could with you under the circumstances. I was trying to keep you from getting hurt."

Angela's eyes stung with unshed tears. She could make no sense out of her mother's angry words. She was exhausted, her head was throbbing, and her whole body was wracked with pain. More than anything, she wanted her mother to leave.

And just like that, her prayers were answered when Jimmy pushed open the door that had been partially open and stepped into her room.

He took in the look on Angela's face and then said, "I think you need to leave now." It wasn't a request.

"I'm not finished talking to my daughter."

Jimmy's green eyes darkened like angry thunderclouds as he said, "Oh, yes, you are."

CHAPTER 32

"I'm sorry. I know Kathy's your mother, but no one has the right to make you cry," Jimmy said, quickly moving toward Angela.

"Thank you. I couldn't take any more from her today. It's so sad she's the way she is. Nothing ever makes her happy. I thought having money would do it, but she never seems to have enough, and she's gone from husband to husband and boyfriend to boyfriend. Now it appears fame is what she's looking for."

Jimmy took hold of her hand and sat on the edge of her bed, wiping the tears from her eyes. "I'll put her back in the no-fly zone," he smiled warmly.

"My grandmother told me my grandfather spoiled my mother because they'd been married almost nineteen years before Kathy was born. They hadn't expected to have any children. He adored his daughter, never held her responsible for her actions, and gave her everything she wanted."

"Where is he now?"

"He was a heavy smoker and passed away from pancreatic cancer when Kathy was in high school. After his death, my grandmother tried unsuccessfully to undo the damage he'd done."

She gave Jimmy a pensive look and said, "I bet you're wondering why Kathy kept me, since she obviously didn't want to be a mother."

"It is strange, yeah."

"When I was younger, I overheard an argument between Kathy and my grandmother. She wanted a certain boy to marry her, and purposefully getting pregnant seemed the way to trap him. He fooled her when he walked away after I was born and never looked back. My grandmother was angry and warned her not to try that stunt again. I ran outside because I didn't want to hear the rest."

Jimmy was quiet, and Angela said, "Don't feel sorry for me. I've had a great life. I've had a few bumps, but who hasn't? My grandmother loved me. You and Matt love me. It doesn't matter that my mother and father don't. Life is good."

Jimmy moved closer and gathered her into her arms. Try as she might, she couldn't stop the tears running down her face.

∽

Angela, walking with relative ease, strolled down the hall, chatting with Jimmy's father. He walked beside her as she pushed the IV pole ahead of them. She was on her third day of post-op and felt better every day. She wasn't expecting them to place Matt in her room when he came out of the ICU. He would need much more care than she did, but it would have been nice and much easier on poor Jimmy and his parents.

She was grateful for Larry and Sandra. Since Larry was self-employed, he could take time away from his work to come by and visit Matt and take Angela for a walk. He was such a sweet, patient man, and it made her realize how much she'd missed not having a father. She wondered if her father ever thought about the baby girl he'd walked away from.

"Are you hurting? Want to go back?" Larry said.

"Oh, no, I'm okay. We can go to the end of the hall and then turn back. I was thinking how lucky Jimmy is to have you and Sandra."

"You know his brother, Sam, would be here too, except he's out of the country with his firm. He'll be back in the States this weekend. You'll get to meet him then."

"Are he and Jimmy alike?"

"Some ways, yes; some ways, no. They look alike, but Sam was always the bookworm, and Jimmy was the athlete. Not that Jimmy didn't do well in school."

"Is Sam married? I'm ashamed to say I've never asked Jimmy. I can't wait to meet him, and I imagine it will mean a lot to Jimmy for his brother to be here."

"He's had many girlfriends, but he never found the one. He and Jimmy were very close as kids, but with both of their careers, they have seen little of each other. But when they get together, it's as if they're kids again."

They stopped in front of her room, and once inside, she carefully eased into a chair. "I think I'll sit here for a few minutes and catch my breath. Thanks for my walk."

"You betcha."

∼

ANGELA HEARD the clicking of heels coming down the hall and instantly knew who it was. Sure enough, Hollywood breezed into the room, flashing a big smile, and carrying a bag. "Sorry I didn't get here yesterday. You know how life can be."

She placed the bag at the foot of the bed and said, "Better late than never."

"I wasn't in a hurry, but you're such a doll for bringing me the album."

"You've got more color in your face today. How are you feeling?" Hollywood asked, taking a seat in the other chair in the room.

"Pretty good. Tired. I just got back from a walk with Larry, and it gets a little bit easier every day. Tell me about Patches and the other dogs. Everything running smoothly?"

"Patches is missing Matt and Jimmy, but she's happy enough. There's always something going on. Had to call a plumber for some stopped-up pipes. I probably need to do a complete remodel, but I'd have to deprive the babies of a home away from home while I do that."

"Maybe you could do it during a slow time. As I remember, you aren't that busy in the early spring and late fall. What if you got more help to take some time off? How long has it been since you've had a vacation?"

"Where in the world would I go? What would I do with myself?"

"Oh, I don't know, take a cruise? I bet your doctor friend would like to go with you."

"You've been talking to Dena, haven't you?"

"I have, but not about you. I love you, Hollywood. You're too young to be old, and life is short. I've spent lots of time lying in that bed and thinking, and that's my conclusion."

Hollywood got up and kissed her on the forehead. "I love you like you were my own. I'll think about what you said. Call me if you need to discuss what's in that photo album."

"I will. I promise. Can you hand it to me before you leave?"

Angela closed her eyes and opened the old album to the first page. She looked so young in her one-piece bathing suit on the beach. It was the summer she'd met Dean. She was glamming for the camera with Dean's arm slung around her shoulders, a wide grin on his face. It wasn't a closeup, but it was obvious how handsome he was, even from a distance.

She couldn't remember who'd taken the picture and hadn't thought about that day in years. Not even when she had gone to the beach with Jimmy and Matt. She and Dean had gone to the beach often. Neither of them had any money, and it was an inexpensive date.

She kept flipping the pages until she found the photo she sought. It was a closeup of Dean wearing his baseball uniform. He'd removed his cap, and his dark curly hair flopped onto his brow. His deep-set coffee-colored eyes were smiling.

She slammed the album closed, afraid of where her thoughts were taking her. She'd put her memories of Dean away and didn't need a picture to remind her of the special place he would always have in her heart. But now she had a fresh reminder.

"Angela," she heard Jimmy's voice from the door. "What's the matter?'

She looked up and quickly blinked away the tears. "Nothing. I'm fine."

"Are you in pain? Do you want me to get the nurse?"

"No, no, I'm okay, really. It seems like all I've done around you is cry."

"That's not true. You're the bravest person I know."

"I want to see Matt. Will they let me see him?"

"Well sure. I'll make it happen."

Thirty minutes later, she was in a wheelchair, her IV pole rolling beside her as Jimmy pushed her into the ICU. With Jimmy's help, she stood beside Matt and studied his sweet face as if seeing him for the first time. His thick dark lashes fanned his eyes, and they lit up with joy when he opened them.

"Angela, hi." He reached for her hand and said, "The doctor said your liver's working great. Thanks."

"My pleasure, sweetheart. She looked at him for the longest time as her heart swelled with pride and love. She looked up at Jimmy and then down at Matt.

Tears flooded her eyes as she wondered, *How will I ever tell them?*

CHAPTER 33

*A*ngela waited in a wheelchair in front of the hospital while Jimmy went to get the car. She shielded her eyes to gaze up at the blue sky and inhaled the welcome scent of flowers, trees, and fresh air that had been so lacking in the sterile hospital atmosphere. She rested her hand on the thick packet of discharge instructions on her lap.

The sound of a news van pulling up and screeching to a stop startled her. Then she saw a sharply dressed woman step out with a microphone in her hand. Fortunately, Jimmy had thought ahead, and the security guard he'd hired jumped in front of Angela and held the newswoman at bay. A second van pulled up within moments, and a crowd of onlookers gathered.

Angela cringed at the barrage of questions the reporters hurled at her. "Is it true you are James Ross's girlfriend? Why did you agree to donate part of your liver? Were you paid for donating? Is it true you and your mother will be on the Today Show?"

When Jimmy's car pulled into the patients' pickup lane,

two hospital security guards joined Marcus to prevent the reporters' access to Angela and Jimmy.

Marcus helped Angela into the front seat and then slid into the back. "I guess there's a mole at the hospital who let the reporters know when you were leaving, ma'am. I'm sorry, Mr. Ross."

"You handled it well, Marcus. I suspected something like this would happen." Jimmy reached across the seat and gently touched Angela's shoulder. "You okay?"

"Yeah. A little surprised, I guess. I forget you're a famous baseball player, not just Jimmy Ross."

"Retired baseball player and I'm not that famous. It must be a slow news week."

She chuckled and gave him a warm smile while berating herself for being a coward. She had said nothing about her suspicions that Matt could be her son. What if she was totally wrong? All she was basing it on was how much he favored Dean and the color of his eyes. It could only be wishful thinking and stir up a hornet's nest for nothing. Jimmy had enough to worry about. He didn't need to know right now.

Maybe she didn't really want to know either. After all, she and Jimmy were together. Matt was in her life. That wouldn't change, even if things didn't work out with Jimmy. She was a part of Matt now, and they would always be connected.

"You ready to go home?"

"Oh, yes, I am," Angela said, and she noticed he was referring to his house as if it were her home, too. Jimmy had talked her into staying at his house until she could care for herself completely. Angela had balked when he'd contracted with a nursing service to be there with her. Still, he'd convinced her by saying she could evaluate the personalities and skill levels of the home care nurses before Matt was discharged in three or four more days.

When they arrived, Sandra and a middle-aged woman wearing scrubs were waiting at Jimmy's house. The woman immediately took charge and said, "Miss Michaels, I'm Retta, and I'm here to help you get better. Let's get you into bed. I imagine the trip home was exhausting."

She led Angela down the hall to a spare bedroom across from the guest room where Matt would recover until he could climb the stairs to his own bedroom. She could see a queen size bed, a television mounted on the wall, and an adjoining bathroom. Retta helped her to bed and arranged her pillows. "You look all wrung out. Why don't you take a nice nap, and I'll be within earshot if you need me."

Jimmy sat down on the bed and said, "I'm sorry. I've got to get back to Matt. Nurse Retta comes with recommendations from Shane and Dena, so I know you'll be in excellent hands."

"Thank you. I could have gone to my house, you know. You didn't need to do all this."

His eyebrows shot up, and he shook his head in disbelief. "All this? Good Lord, woman, you saved my son's life. I can never repay you. Taking care of you is the least I can do." He leaned down and whispered, "Besides, I'm crazy about you. I'll see you sometime tomorrow." He gave her a lingering kiss and waved as he left.

∼

JIMMY'S FOOTSTEPS abruptly stopped when he entered Matt's room and discovered a man sitting in a chair facing the bed. When the man turned around, Jimmy's apprehension turned to joy. "Sam! You aren't supposed to be here until tomorrow."

"Oh, well then, do you want me to leave and come back?"

Matt laughed as he watched his dad embrace his brother,

Sam, in a fierce hug and said, "Man, am I glad to see you. How long can you stay?"

"Through the weekend. I'm staying with Mom and Pop, but I want to meet Angela. Matt told me she went home today."

"Yeah, to my house. I hired a nurse to be there with her and Matt when he gets home."

"Is she pretty, Dad?" Matt asked.

Sam winked at Matt and said, "Yeah, Jimmy, is she pretty?"

"Sorry, tiger," Jimmy said to his son. "She's too old for both of us."

Later, after Matt fell asleep, Sam said, "You look like hell, Jimmy. You getting any sleep at all?"

"Sure," Jimmy said, then admitted, "Well, truthfully, no, not a lot. The fold-down sofa isn't ideal for my less-than-perfect back."

"Yeah, years of tossing a tiny ball at ninety miles an hour will do that to you. And I don't suppose worrying about Matt has anything to do with your sleep problems either?"

"I haven't said this to anyone else, but I lie there most of the night listening to him breathe. I'm scared to death something will go wrong. All kinds of complications can happen after surgery, infection, excess bleeding, the graft might not take, or his body could reject the organ."

"Stop! You're making my head hurt. Has any of that happened?"

"No, of course not. The doctors are pleased with everything. I guess I'm borrowing trouble, as Mom would say."

Sam shrugged his shoulders. "I'm not a father, Jim. I have no idea what the proper reaction should be, but since I'm in San Diego for a couple of days, let me help. I can stay right here, and you can go home and get some actual sleep for a few hours. Matt will be fine with me."

Jimmy looked uncertain and finally said, "I could use a shower and change of clothes, and yeah, some proper sleep. Thanks, bro."

~

WHEN HE GOT HOME, Jimmy checked in with Retta, who reported that Angela had eaten a bowl of soup for lunch and had just fallen asleep after a short walk around the backyard. Jimmy took a shower, shaved, and changed clothes. Then he carefully slid into bed next to Angela, and for the first time since Matt's surgery, he fell into a deep sleep.

When he opened his eyes, Angela was looking at him. He reached out and touched her lovely, smiling face. "Hi," he said. He had noticed a difference in her for the last couple of days. It was nothing he could put his finger on. She had become quiet, more reserved, and not her usual self. She was probably uncomfortable but didn't want to worry anyone, so she'd chosen not to complain.

"Hi. What are you doing here? Who's with Matt?"

"When I got back to the hospital, my brother Sam was there. He insisted I come home and get some sleep. He rather bluntly told me I looked like hell."

"Oh, how nice that he's here for you and Matt. I think you look very handsome, and you smell good, too."

"Thank you. I took a long shower and shaved." He ran his fingers through her hair and said, "You smell like roses."

"Retta helped me take a shower and wash my hair. I feel human and feminine again."

"You're always beautiful to me, Angel. He wondered what it would be like to wake up with her beside him every day. Jimmy thought they needed to discuss that possibility after she and Matt recovered and regained their strength.

"Retta said you took a walk and ate lunch. You act like you're feeling better."

"It's nice to be in an actual bed without all the hospital noises. Why don't you help me sit up, and we can walk into the kitchen? Your mom stocked the fridge, so I'm sure we can find you something to eat."

Yes, he thought, having Angela here in his life every day would be very nice indeed.

CHAPTER 34

Jimmy and Angela lay on chaise lounges under the back porch canopy, enjoying cold glasses of lemonade and the fresh air. It had been three weeks since Angela had been discharged from the hospital.

Matt was home now, too, and asleep in his room under Retta's watchful eye. Patches was exploring the bushes in the yard and walking without a limp. Angela had arranged for her neighbor to water the flowers at her house, and Jimmy hired a lawn service company to mow the yard.

Jimmy reached for Angela's hand and kissed it. "You getting cabin fever?"

"A little. I spoke with my boss. He suggested I come back to work next week on a part-time basis. No lifting, of course, and no standing on my feet for a long time, which rules out performing surgery, but I think doing exams will be good for me."

Jimmy had been out of the house most of the day while filming a commercial endorsement spot for a local car dealership and then meeting with his agent. Although retired,

Jimmy was still in high demand, even more so since the news of Matt's illness leaked out.

"My agent wants me to do a brief interview with one of the news outlets about Matt. He says all kinds of stories are circulating and wants to give me the opportunity to speak about it on my terms."

"Not with that horrible woman who stuck her microphone in my face, I hope?"

"No, this interview is with a national news reporter, and there will be no mention of you except to say that Matt received his liver from a live donor. The piece will mostly discuss my plans after retirement and give an update on Matt's health."

"Okay. I appreciate you keeping my name out of it."

"I know what a private person you are, and I would never try to exploit you."

Jimmy got up and moved to the cushion next to Angela. He cupped her face with his oversized, calloused hands and looked into her eyes for the longest time. Finally, he said, "You look beautiful, and I love you. When did the doctor say it was okay to fool around?"

Angela laughed and pulled him down for a kiss. A long, passionate kiss. "As soon as I feel like it."

"And do you feel like it?"

"Kiss me again, and I'll let you know."

His mouth swooped down to capture hers, and then he took her hand as they walked through a patio door that led directly into the master bedroom. He locked the door after turning on the sound system to play soft guitar music and leaving Patches in the hallway.

Angela sat on the edge of the bed and slipped off the baggy shorts and loose blouse she'd been wearing sans underwear.

"Why, Angela Michaels, you've gone commando." He laughed as he stripped off his own clothes.

"They're too confining right now, and fastening my bra is too hard."

"I'd be happy to help you with that anytime." He wiggled his eyebrows and slid into bed beside her. "Seriously, we don't have to do anything. I'm happy just to hold you again. I've missed being close to you like this."

"Me too," she said, putting her arms around his neck while snuggling against his warm body.

∼

JIMMY LAY NEXT TO ANGELA, gently ran his fingers through her silky, long, dark hair, and felt at peace for the first time in weeks. He knew the feeling was only a partial reprieve because Matt still had a long recovery ahead of him, but his son was getting better every day, and Angela, well, Angela was amazing.

"You awake?" he asked, kissing the top of her head and inhaling the fresh scent of her strawberry shampoo.

"Yes, although I'm pretty comfortable, so I might nod off any minute."

"Before you do, I want to talk to you about something. Please think about it before you say no."

"Okay, this sounds serious. What do you want to talk about?"

"First, you should know that I already talked to Matt. He thinks it's a terrific idea. I explained exactly what it would mean, and he said he's almost thirteen now and not a dummy."

"What are you talking about? The suspense is killing me."

"I want you to move in with me. With us."

"I'm already moved in with you."

"Don't be obtuse. I want us to live together in this house, with your clothes in the closet and your toothbrush next to mine. I want you in my bed every night."

"But what about my house, furniture, and things?" She sounded anxious. "I love my flowers and my pergola."

"You don't have to do anything with your house right away, and you can bring anything you want here. Grow your flowers here, and we can build another pergola."

He waited for a response, and when there was none, he said, "I love you, Angela. I want to be with you every day."

She slowly turned toward him and said, "I'm sorry. I love you too, and being here with you has spoiled me. I've never lived with anyone since my freshman year of college. I might drive you crazy. What if I leave my wet towels on the floor or my dirty dishes in the sink?"

"I've seen your house. I know how you live, and besides, as you know, I have a housekeeping service that comes once a week."

He sat up abruptly and reached for his clothes. "I'm getting the feeling you're finding any excuse you can to keep from moving in with me. I'd never expect you to do something you don't want to do. I believe that's the reason you sent old Greg boy packing."

"That's not fair. I didn't love Greg, and I do love you. But I'm afraid, okay?"

"Afraid of what? I won't try to change you or run your life."

"It's not that. What if something happens to you, or we break up? I haven't had a serious relationship since I was sixteen, and that one didn't turn out so good."

"I'm not going to die, Angela," he said, calmer now as he sat back down on the bed and carefully took her into his arms. "And I'm never going to leave you."

Trust didn't come easily for Angela. He could see that

now. She was dealing with leftovers from a neglectful childhood. He wondered what other things besides neglect her mother had put her through.

Hé was offering her a chance to live in a luxurious house in a prestigious neighborhood, but that status meant nothing to her. And when had it ever meant that much to him? He had been raised in a middle-class family. His father still worked as an electrician, although Jimmy had tried several times to get him to retire.

His late wife was from a wealthy family, so when he signed his first multimillion-dollar contract, he tried to give her the life she was used to. She had wealthy friends and worked in a prestigious law firm. During the off-season, they had socialized with the rich and sometimes famous. But since Cindy's death, he seldom saw any of those people. They were her friends, not his.

The two women were nearly exact opposites in looks and temperament. Cindy was tall, curvy, and blonde, while Angela was brunette and petite. Cindy was the life of the party, and Angela was reserved, but not shy.

His heart had said goodbye to Cindy the night he told Angela he loved her. He was ready for a committed relationship, but now he wondered if she felt the same. Maybe she wasn't ready to say goodbye to Dean. He felt bad about pushing her too fast.

Overwhelmed by a mix of regret and guilt, he felt a lump forming in his throat. He was scared, unsure of where things were going and what the future held. "Angela, I'm sorry if I put too much pressure on you. I just want you to know that I'm here for you, no matter what you decide," he said, trying to keep his voice steady. "I understand if you don't feel the same way, I just want you to know that I care about you and your happiness. If it's the house you don't like, we could always move to another one. I want you to feel comfortable."

She touched his arm, and he turned to gaze into the depths of those beautiful brown eyes. "I'm sorry, Jimmy. I'm an idiot. Change is hard, and it's doubly hard for me to depend on anyone. But I love you so much, and I want to be with you, too. Please be patient with me. I promise not to leave my towels on the floor."

"Is that a yes?"

Her lips brushed against his as she said, "Yes."

CHAPTER 35

It was chilly as Angela and Matt strolled down the sidewalk past the spacious, sprawling homes in the neighborhood. Patches walked obediently beside Matt. After Jimmy asked her to move in with him over a month earlier, she moved into Jimmy's house from the guest room where she had been recovering from surgery. Just as he wished, her clothes were in his closet, and her toothbrush was next to his.

Matt would return to school right after Thanksgiving break, which was just around the corner. Angela didn't much care for holidays, having spent most of them alone. While in college, friends had invited her to their homes, and later the receptionist at the emergency clinic asked her to come for a holiday dinner.

Instead of accepting these kind invitations, she'd begged off. In college, she used the excuse that she needed to study, and more recently, Angela had told Rachel she was working holiday shifts for extra money. Hollywood had always invited her. Still, she declined, not wanting to intrude on a big Madden family gathering.

ANGEL'S HEART

This year, she would go with Jimmy to his parents' house, and his brother would be there. She'd finally found the family she'd never had, and life looked wonderful. But guilt nagged at her since she had still not told Jimmy what she suspected about Matt.

It was funny that in all the time she'd spent with Jimmy and Matt, she'd never once asked the date of Matt's birthday. She didn't want to know. What if it was THE date? Wouldn't that cement her suspicions?

Matt looked up at her with his big eyes shining with happiness, even after everything he'd been through the past few months. "The doctors said I can probably start swimming and riding my bike next week after my checkup."

"I know, your dad told me. I can do that too. Maybe we can all go for a bike ride together. Are you eager to get back to school?"

"I'll say. And I'll be playing baseball by spring."

She tousled his hair and said, "I can't wait to see you play and pitch just like your dad."

"Well, yeah, that's really cool. Especially since I'm adopted. So, I did it all on my own with some great coaching, of course."

Angela's stomach knotted, and she had a hard time swallowing. "Yeah, seventh-grade baseball. Your team will play other schools. That will be fun."

Angela's hands suddenly started to sweat. She cleared her throat and asked, "When will you be thirteen?"

"March twentieth," he said, picking up the pace as if being propelled toward that date.

Angela's throat was dry, her heart pounded, and she felt faint. "Can we slow down for a minute? I think I overdid it."

"You okay? Want to turn around?" Matt said, his face stricken with worry.

Tears gathered in her eyes, and she was glad she had worn

dark sunglasses. It was time. She couldn't keep this from Jimmy or Matt any longer. "Yeah, I'm okay now, but I think we should go back."

∼

MATT SAT at the kitchen table with the homeschool teacher, who came to the house three days a week to work with him on the basic seventh-grade curriculum. Jimmy tried to be home for the lessons, but his agent kept him busy for a retired guy. He'd missed their morning walk today.

The baseball organization had approached him about working with them. He was open to the idea if the position didn't require traveling. He'd been away from his son too often as a player and wasn't interested in doing that again. Maybe some role in the front office would be interesting. He had plenty of time to decide. For now, he was content to be home with Matt and Angela.

Angela was an easy person to be around. She did not ask for changes to the house, even though his late wife had done all the decorating. She'd added a few possessions from her home, but not enough to make a huge difference. This kind, lovely woman had seamlessly slipped into their lives. Jimmy was content and blissfully happy for the first time in years, and Matt basked in the glow of Angela's nurturing attention.

Angela had returned to the emergency clinic part-time and managed to keep up with the physical demands, although he could tell she was exhausted after her shift.

She breezed into the room, looking fresh from a nap and ready for work. "I won't be late tonight. I need to talk to you about something when I get home."

"Let's talk now," he said, leaning forward to put his arm around her waist.

She smiled and shook her head. "No, I don't have time. It's a little complicated."

"Should I be worried? You're not second-guessing us, are you?" When he stood up, there were only inches between them. He lifted her chin to kiss her and was relieved when she warmly kissed him back.

"No, Jimmy. It's something I found out today, and we need to talk about it. I love you, and that will never change."

Grinning, he said, "Ditto, kiddo."

After she left for work, Matt was tired of doing schoolwork and settled in to watch a movie. Jimmy decided it was the perfect time to tackle something he had been putting off for years. After Cindy's death, his mother packed up all of Cindy's personal items. They moved them to the attic with all her files from the law firm.

Jimmy felt holding on to Cindy's things was no longer appropriate since he had started a permanent relationship with Angela. It was time. All her jewelry was in a safe deposit box for now. He would give it to Matt when he was older if he wanted to give some pieces to a special woman in his life.

His house was a colonial with dormer windows and an enormous attic that could easily be converted into a bedroom. He unlocked the hallway door and walked up the stairs. After Cindy died, his mother had labeled the contents of the boxes in her neat handwriting, and he and his brother had neatly stacked them. He hadn't been up here since.

Jimmy opened a window to let in some fresh air which did little to dispel the musty odor and film of fine dust. He quickly glanced at the boxes labeled as clothing items and set them aside. Then he found the ones marked as personal office items that her law firm had packed and sent over. He sat on the floor, cut through the packing tape, and opened the lid. Inside were a mouse pad, paper clip holders, scissors, and typical items Cindy kept on her desk. He would let Matt go through it later and decide if he wanted anything.

The next box contained files from Cindy's personal notes on clients. Any legal documents were kept by the firm. He was about to set it aside for shredding when he saw a manilla folder with the word ADOPTION. He pulled it out, looked at the legal document, and started to read. Even with the overhead bulb, the light was poor, so he pulled his cell from his pocket, clicked on the flashlight, and shined it on the legal paper.

Bile rose in his throat as he read the words in dark type. PRIVATE ADOPTION AGREEMENT. His heart raced as he took the folder and hurried down the stairs. He checked on Matt, who was still engrossed in the movie, and brought him a cold bottle of water. After locking the door in his home office, he turned on the desk lamp and settled in to read the folder's contents.

The document was written in formal legalese, and he read it carefully line-by-line while becoming more confused and shocked by the minute. How could he have been so blind? How could this be true?

He was finding it difficult to process this information. Why would she do this to him? The knowledge of the significant financial transaction involved and the decision to adopt a child under these terms without his knowledge or agreement were overwhelming.

By the time he reached the end of the document, he was physically ill and barely made it into the bathroom to empty the contents of his stomach. After washing his face and rinsing his mouth, he returned to the desk.

Just then, Matt tapped on the glass of the French doors. Jimmy shoved the folder into the top desk drawer and opened the door to see Matt and Patches standing there. "You okay, buddy?" he asked his son.

"Yeah, but Patches needs a nap. She's been racing around the backyard doing zoomies, and she's all wiped out."

Jimmy smiled at his words. He knew that Matt frequently attributed his own emotions and distress to his dog, making it easier for him to admit his feelings. Matt was becoming impatient with how slow his recovery was going. The doctors were pleased, but Matt wanted to be an energetic preteen again, without limitations and restrictions.

"I can see that. Maybe you better take Patches up to your room and let her rest for a bit. She'll have more energy when she wakes up."

~

As soon as he was alone, Jimmy pulled out the folder and reread the document. He took notes on a legal pad to clarify what he had learned and to write it in plain English.

- Cindy Ross had drawn up legal documents for a private adoption.
- Cindy Ross did not tell her husband the terms of the adoption.
- Cindy Ross signed the adoption papers and forged James Ross's signature.
- The terms of the adoption were that Cindy Ross would pay the birth mother three-hundred-thousand dollars for her medical and living expenses.
- The birth mother's name was Angela Michaels.

Jimmy inhaled deeply as he wrote the last line. He couldn't grasp the magnitude of the betrayal he had experienced by both women he loved. Overcome with grief and loss, he felt violated as a growing sense of anger raged within him.

CHAPTER 36

Angela rehearsed the words she would say to Jimmy as she drove home from the clinic. How would he react? Would he believe her or think she was lying and insist on DNA testing? She had no idea. If only she had mentioned her suspicions when she first suspected Matt was her child. Maybe it would have been easier. But the timing wasn't right then, and it was too late now.

When she got home, she went straight upstairs. One more look at Matt would give her courage. Matt was already asleep when she peeked into his room. She tucked the covers around him and then went to the den, where she expected to find Jimmy watching sports on TV. He wasn't there. She walked through the spacious house while softly calling out his name.

She finally found him sitting on the back porch with a beer bottle in his hand and three empty ones sitting on the small table. He must have heard her footsteps and turned toward her. She could not define his expression, but it made her shiver. "What is it? Did something happen?" Her first thought was of Matt, but she knew he was fast asleep, looking like an angel.

Jimmy's voice rumbled and slurred when he said, "You tell me," and handed her several pages of legal paper.

"What's this?" She took the papers in her hand, turned on the lamp, and sank into a chair. Her heart pounded, and her knees felt weak. She knew Jimmy didn't drink, or at least not to excess. Something was terribly wrong.

"You don't remember?" he said sarcastically.

"No, I've never seen this before."

"Enough with the lies, Angela. Between you and my wife, I've had a lifetime of them." His voice was raw and harsh.

Angela flipped through the pages and began to tremble with fear as she read the words saying she'd sold her baby to Cindy Ross for three hundred thousand dollars. She sucked in her breath when she saw her name scrawled across the page.

"There is some mistake. I didn't do this. That's not even my signature."

"And here I thought you were so noble in getting scholarships and working your way through school. You must not handle money well since you drive around in a crappy car and make everyone think you're barely making ends meet. Maybe you should have asked for more money when you sold your baby." He finished his beer and watched the bottle explode into a million pieces as he threw it across the cement.

Angela had always been slow to anger. The practice had served her well since she had to deal with a sociopath for a mother, but hearing the man she loved say vicious things to her in a cruel, biting tone was her breaking point. "Okay, that's it. Stop talking. You're drunk and in no mood to listen to anything I would say to you."

Ignoring her, he continued, but there was a change in his

tone. He sounded hurt and sad. "How'd you plan it, huh? How did you worm your way into Matt's life and make him love you? Make me fall in love with you. You're an evil woman, Angela Michaels. A regular chip off the old block."

After the way he spoke to her, Angela knew she should have walked out, but she couldn't ignore the misery she saw in his eyes. "While I was in the hospital, I had a dream that made me suspect Matt was my son, but I wasn't sure until today. That's what I wanted to talk to you about tonight. The rest of this is garbage." She shook the papers and tossed them in his lap. "I don't know what kind of agreement your wife and my mother had, but it was never with my permission."

He seemed to sober up a bit as he said, "I'll always be grateful for what you did for Matt, but I've already lived with one woman who lied to me. I'm not going through that again. I suppose you'll want to tell Matt who you are since that was your game all along. All I ask is that you let me talk to him first."

Tears rushed into Angela's eyes, and she clenched her fists, wanting to hurl herself at this man she loved and beat some sense into him. This man didn't love her enough or know her well enough to trust her. He branded her a liar without giving her a chance to explain.

She stood, straightened her shoulders, and said, "Goodbye, Jimmy," as she walked into the house.

He was right behind her, grabbing her arm. "What about Matt? What are you going to tell him?"

She shrugged her arm loose and said, "Let me go! I won't tell him anything." She opened the front door and ran to her car as tears threatened to blind her. Gulping deep breaths to calm herself, she drove toward the one person left on this earth who had always believed in her.

Hollywood Madden knew heartbreak when she saw it. Angela was crying so hard that her chest was heaving, and it took a long time for her to settle down enough to talk. Hollywood gave her water to drink, put a throw around her shoulders, and pulled her into a bear hug. They sat together on the sofa until Angela was calm enough to talk.

When Angela was ready to talk, she began pacing and pouring her heart out to Hollywood. "Do you think my mother had the adoption for money planned all along? The whole time I was pregnant?"

Hollywood knew this was no time to remain neutral. "I certainly think so. Maybe that's why she wouldn't let me see you when you were in the hospital. She had this plan all worked out, and she was afraid I might figure it out. I always wondered why she went to baseball games and got so chummy with James Ross's wife."

∼

Angela left Hollywood's home after pouring her heart out and crying a bucket of tears until she was all wrung out. Her eyes were swollen, and she felt like crap, but she was on a mission now, and her mother was the target.

When she pulled into the driveway, she saw that all the lights were out. That could mean anything. Kathy wasn't home. Kathy was home but otherwise occupied with her current lover. Or, shock of all shocks, Kathy was asleep.

Angela slammed her car door, rushed to the door, and leaned on the bell. She heard the chimes echoing from inside. Then she pounded on the door like a crazy woman. "Open the door, Kathy, before your neighbors come out, so I can tell them what you did."

The door swung open, and Kathy stood there with her hair in disarray and her face devoid of makeup. "Angela, what are you doing here screaming at my front door?" Kathy grabbed Angela and pulled her inside.

"I know what you did, Kathy. I just want to know the reason why."

She could tell her mother was nervous, and her voice shook as she said, "What are you raving about? And what's with calling me Kathy? I'm your mother."

"I no longer have a mother, not after what you did. You sold my son, your grandson, for money. Three hundred thousand dollars, to be exact. That's how you could live high after I left home for school. No wonder you were so afraid I would get together with Jimmy. You were afraid I'd find out, and then all your snooty friends would know what you did."

Kathy slapped Angela hard and said, "You have no right to talk to me that way. I am your mother. I didn't get rid of you when I could have, and believe me, I sacrificed every day because of that decision."

"I believe that's the first honest emotion you've ever shown me except for indifference. I know all about why you kept me, Kathy. You thought you could get my father to marry you. And the joke was on you because it didn't work, did it? He didn't want either of us."

"That's not true," Kathy said, her face red with rage. "It's you he didn't want."

"Did you think I didn't know how you cheated me?"

"Of course, you didn't know because I have done nothing wrong."

"No, Kathy. I'm talking about Grandma's house now. Did you think I didn't know you forged my name on Grandma's house deed, so you could sell it out from under me? That I didn't know she left me everything because she loved me. I recognized that same forgery on a legal document you signed. That's a felony, Kathy."

Angela caught her breath, ready for another round, as she

said, "I knew, Kathy. I knew you stole my inheritance from my grandmother, but I let you because you were my mother, and you gave birth to me. I thought I owed you. But I can never forgive you for stealing and selling my baby, your flesh and blood. I didn't know what was happening because I was so sick, and then you lied to me afterward."

"You're talking crazy, and you were sick and weak. That's why your signature didn't look the same. You can't prove a thing."

"Oh yes, I can. Tonight, Jimmy showed me a legal document signed by Cindy Ross with a signature that's definitely not mine."

Stumbling over her words, Kathy said, "That woman said she wouldn't tell her husband. It would stay between us."

"Well, well, the story gets better and better. It would make a great one for your friend on Channel 8. I think I'll call her up and give her a scoop."

Angela stepped forward and looked straight into Kathy's eyes. "I never want to see you or hear from you again. You are dead to me."

As she walked toward her car, Angela heard her mother say, "The joke's on you because I'll never tell you who your father is now. Your real father doesn't even know you're alive."

Angela let the words roll off her like she did everything her mother said and started the engine. A sense of calm resolve enveloped her as she resolved to go on alone. She was fine before she met Jimmy and Matt, and although it would take time, she would be fine again. Knowing her baby was loved and cared for was all that mattered. She knew one thing for sure. She would never fall in love again.

CHAPTER 37

Jimmy groaned and awoke with a splitting headache and the remnants of a nightmare. He rolled over, reached out his arm, and suddenly realized he hadn't been dreaming. Angela was gone. He recalled the vicious words he'd spat at her last night after she'd admitted to being Matt's mother but denied everything else he had accused her of.

Why should he believe her? She was a liar, just like Cindy. Cindy knew he would never have agreed to buy a woman's baby, and that's exactly why she hadn't told him. How can you have a marriage built on secrets and lies?

She said a client at work had a daughter who wanted to give her baby a loving home. The birth mother was uninsured, so all she asked of the adopting family was for them to pay her hospital bills. Jimmy remembered writing checks for those bills, but the side deal was all Cindy's doing.

Something about the whole situation nagged at him. He couldn't believe that Angela was that conniving at sixteen. Her mother must have put her up to it.

Jimmy stumbled into the kitchen like a blind man and reached for the carafe. It was empty. Angela always made the coffee in the morning, and she was gone. He felt like screaming cuss words at the world, but he bit them back when Matt came into the kitchen.

"Hey kid, how are you feeling?"

"Good. Where's Angela?" Matt said, looking around the kitchen as if expecting her to walk in.

"Uh, she had to work," Jimmy said nervously. This was the first time Jimmy deliberately lied to his son, but he couldn't ever tell him the horrible truth that his biological mother had sold him.

"Oh, that's weird. She wasn't feeling good when we went for a walk yesterday, so I thought she'd stay home today and rest."

"I'm sorry I missed that walk yesterday. What'd you guys talk about?"

"Baseball, riding bikes, and school. She asked me when I'd be thirteen. She's easy to talk to, you know. Then she said she'd overdone it on the walk, and we came back home."

After breakfast, Matt settled in to do his schoolwork. Jimmy retreated to his office and took the disturbing legal papers from his desk drawer to read them again. This time, he tried to keep his emotions at bay. It didn't work. His stomach still turned over at the sight of Angela's name. Then he remembered her voice as she insisted, "This isn't even my signature."

He picked up his phone and called her cell, but it went directly to voicemail. Trying to keep all emotion out of his voice, he said, "Angela, this is Jimmy. We need to talk." Next, he called the clinic, but the receptionist said she wasn't scheduled to work that day. Finally, he looked up the number for Hollywood's Kennel and waited on hold until someone said she could not come to the phone.

"Shit," he said, slamming his cell on the desk. What a monumental mess he'd made of things. He hadn't even given Angela a chance to explain herself. Would it have made a difference?

When his doorbell rang, his heart jumped as Patches barked and ran excitedly in circles. Angela was here. What would he say to her? For Matt's sake, he promised himself he would listen. He swung the door open, and a disappointed scowl formed on his face as he said, "Oh, hi, Mom."

"Were you expecting someone else?"

"No, sorry. Come on in." She carried a crock pot and handed it to Jimmy as Patches continued to twirl with excitement.

"I brought a roast, potatoes, and carrots for your dinner tonight. Where's Angela?"

"Hi, Grandma," Matt said as he came down the stairs. "Dad says she's at work," Matt said as he hugged her. "I have a math test tomorrow, so I'm upstairs cramming. What did you bring me?"

"Lots of protein and veggies for supper. Sorry, no sugar. Doctor's orders."

"I know. Love you." He called to Patches, and they both disappeared upstairs.

"It's amazing how resilient he is. He looks great, Jimmy." She hugged him and said, "God was looking out for him when he sent Angela to you. I thought she worked yesterday. Don't let her overdo it, Jimmy. You don't want her to get sick."

He reluctantly met his mother's eyes and said, "She's not at work. We had a fight, and she left."

"That doesn't sound like our Angela. What did you do?"

"I didn't do anything. Let me put the food in the kitchen and get you some coffee. Then we'll go into my office, and I'll explain everything to you."

After Jimmy replayed last night's dramatic episode, his mother pursed her lips, and her eyes filled with tears. "How wonderful for Angela and Matt that she found her baby accidentally after all these years."

"What do you mean? Why are you taking her side? She deliberately set up this whole thing."

Sandra placed her mug of coffee firmly on the end table, sloshing a few drops on the wood. "My, my! She's quite the femme fatale and a sorcerer too. She conjured up the rain and a dog you could run over just so you could take said dog to the clinic and meet her. Now that is quite a feat."

"You saw the adoption agreement."

"Yes, I did, and I believe you told me Angela said it wasn't her signature. Right?"

He nodded, but before he could comment, Sandra continued. "Even if it was, Jimmy, the girl was only sixteen years old. How mature were you at that age? And that mother of hers. I wouldn't trust that woman as far as I could throw her. Why didn't you let Angela explain? Everyone makes mistakes, son. Even you."

~

FIFTEEN MINUTES LATER, he left his mother with Matt and drove away. When he pulled up in front of Angela's house, her car wasn't in the driveway. He knocked on the door anyway and noticed the next-door neighbor glaring at him. "Do you know if Angela is home?" Jimmy yelled across the yard.

"I wouldn't know. I mind my own business."

"If you see her, will you tell her Jimmy came by?"

The woman nodded and continued to water her plants.

His next stop was Hollywood's Kennel, where he was met

with an even colder shoulder than Angela's neighbor had given him. "Well, if it isn't Jimmy Ross, breaker of hearts and all-around ass." Hollywood was blow-drying and brushing out the coat of a standard poodle on the grooming table while the dog chomped on treats.

"Where is she?" He sounded a little desperate, even to himself. "Can you please turn that thing off so you can hear me?"

"She isn't here, and don't yell at me, mister. You're scaring Muffin."

"But you've seen her. Talked to her, right? You're correct about me. I am an ass. I didn't give her a chance to explain. I need to do that for all our sakes."

She set down the blower and gave Muffin another treat, as she said. "You believe that the woman who gave up part of her liver to save a boy's life, a boy she didn't even know very well, would give her own baby over to strangers for an exorbitant amount of money." She paused and took a breath. "It wasn't a question, sonny boy. That's what you believe, right?"

He swallowed hard. After listening to her words, he wasn't so sure of himself anymore. "Why didn't she tell me she knew Matt was her son if she was so innocent? She said she had some kind of dream, and when she woke up, she knew. That's far-fetched."

"You ever see a picture of Dean? Matt's biological father?"

"No, why?"

"Dark curly hair, big deep-set brown eyes. Dean was a whiz at baseball but wanted to be a vet. She asked me to bring her old picture album to the hospital, so she could be sure." Muffin fidgeted, and Hollywood soothed her with another treat. The dog yawned and lay down on the table.

"Angela was torn. She didn't want to tell you what she suspected in case it wasn't true. Yesterday, when she asked

Matt about his birth date, all her suspicions clicked into place. She was going to tell you and let you decide what you wanted to do."

Jimmy sank into a chair and covered his face with his hands. "What about the other stuff?"

"You mean that worthless, trashy woman your dead wife conspired with to steal Angela's baby? You know, or maybe you don't because, after all, you are a man, that Angela almost died when Matt was born. There was no way she could have or would have signed away her baby. That baby was Dean's son, and she loved Dean more than anything."

Hollywood wiped her hands on her jeans and said, "Her witch of a mother wouldn't let me see her right after she gave birth, so I can't tell you exactly what happened. But I know this. If Angela said that wasn't her signature, it wasn't. Kathy is a pathological liar. She stole Angela's inheritance from her grandmother by forging Angela's signature. Why wouldn't she do it again to get thousands of dollars?"

"Wait," he said, holding up his hands. "Angela almost died? She told me she was sick, but I didn't know it was that bad. And Kathy forged her name on an inheritance?"

"Oh, yeah. Who knows what else she's done to that sweet girl? But I can tell you for sure, Angela never had an extra three hundred grand to spend. I know that for a fact. She struggled to stay afloat. Now go away and leave her alone. You've done enough damage."

"Where is she? Please tell me. I must make things right. Ask her to forgive me."

Hollywood sighed and shook her head. "She's at home. She parked her car in the neighbor's garage. I don't think she wants to see you, Jimmy."

"Please don't tell her I'm coming. I need to talk to her."

Hollywood didn't answer and turned the hair dryer on again.

ANGEL'S HEART

~

ANGELA SAT on her back porch under her beloved pergola while drinking a glass of cold water and listening to traffic on the main road. She'd glanced at her phone earlier when Jimmy called, and later she heard him pounding on her door. She had nothing to say to him.

She'd asked her neighbors if she could park her car in their garage for a couple of days. Thankfully, they agreed. She was sure Jimmy would give up soon.

When her doorbell rang again, she heard Jimmy shouting that he knew she was home. Hopefully, one of the neighbors would call the police, but it had to be an emergency in this neighborhood before they would respond.

She lay back on her lawn chair and closed her eyes. They were red and irritated from the hours of crying, and her face was puffy. She thought about leaving San Diego. She'd never been out of California. Maybe she'd move to the South. She'd heard Southerners were warm, friendly people. She knew she couldn't live with the temptation of seeing her son and her ex-lover again.

"Angela!" She heard Jimmy's voice coming from the young couple's backyard next door. She sat up just as he climbed over the fence and landed gracefully, barely missing the Prickly Pear plant. She repressed a smile at the thought that him landing in the thorns would have been poetic justice. She considered going inside and locking herself in the house, but she wasn't that much of a coward.

"I need to talk to you," he said. She saw he hadn't shaved, and his hair was mussed and dirty.

"Now you want to talk. I told you I wouldn't say anything to Matt. Contrary to what you might think, I'm not a liar."

He carefully inched toward her, as if approaching a

frightened animal. "I've been out of my mind since last night. I'm so sorry for the hateful things I said."

"That makes one of us."

"I know you're angry, and I don't blame you. Hollywood told me I was an ass, and so did my mother, only not in those exact words."

"What do you want? You've already broken my heart. What other damage do you want to inflict?"

"I can't use the excuse that Cindy lied to me; therefore, all women lie. So, I won't insult you with that one. I know you're different, and all I can say is that I love you and beg you to forgive me. I probably won't die if you don't, but it's going to be damn hard to live without you."

He sat down on the chaise lounge beside her and wanted to take her in his arms more than anything. Instead, he said, "Is Matt really your son?"

"I'm as sure as I can be without a DNA test. He looks like Dean, and he was born on March 20th. That's when my baby was born, and you have Kathy's and Cindy's agreement. I confronted my mother last night. Of course, she denied it, but she got quite upset when I told her I would call Channel 8 to give them the story."

"I know you wouldn't do that. You would never do anything to hurt Matt."

She let the words hang in the air. They were nice to hear, even if they were a bit late. "No, I wouldn't do that."

"Can you forgive me? Will you forgive me? Come back to me, and I promise I'll take excellent care of you and never doubt you again. I love you, sweetheart. I need you, and so does Matt. I loved Cindy, but in a different way. I can't say I ever needed her or was completely head over heels in love with her like I am with you."

Her eyes were moist as she stood up. She didn't respond,

but she let him pull her into his arms. "I know it will take time, Angel, but please come back to me. To both of us."

"You hurt me, Jimmy. Really hurt me. Will I forgive you? Yes, because that's what you do when you love someone, but it will take a lot longer to forget. You'll have to give me time."

CHAPTER 38

Angela convinced herself that she wasn't lonely. That she didn't miss the man she loved and her precious son, with whom she had so recently bonded. Her recovery from the surgery had gone as scheduled, and she could work at full capacity again. She took every overtime shift they would give her on the Emergency Vet Clinic's schedule and saved as much money as possible. She had decided to sell her car, buy a better one, and head south to start over when she had the funds.

That was her plan, and she was sticking to it. That is until she saw Jimmy Ross waiting by her car after work early one morning after she had pulled an overnight shift. Surprised by the warm glow that flowed through her at the sight of him, her first thought was how tall, handsome, and sexy he was, and her second was to wonder if something was wrong with Matt.

As she drew closer, he smiled, and she saw the crinkles around his beautiful hazel eyes. So, it wasn't about Matt. He looked too relaxed. Why was he here? Before she could ask him, he babbled. "I know I said I'd give you time. I've tried to stay away. Didn't want to bug you at work, but I had to say this in person."

"Say what in person?" She could not stop herself from wondering.

"I want to start over. I'm here with my hat in my hand," he touched his head. "Well, not literally, but I'm here to ask if you will have dinner with me." He paused. "Soon. Whenever you are free."

She hesitated, but not because she was contemplating his invitation. Her answer would be yes because she still loved this man with all her heart. Instead, she was trying to think through her schedule at the clinic. After several minutes of dead silence, Jimmy said, "Angela?"

"I am free tomorrow night if that works for you."

His grin answered for him. "I will make reservations for a wonderful restaurant on the beach. Dress is casual, but the food is elegant. Can I pick you up at six?"

"I'll be ready," she said, turning towards her car.

∼

JIMMY DROVE HOME FEELING SIMULTANEOUSLY ELATED and disappointed. She had said yes to dinner but had not tried to connect with him. She barely met his gaze and behaved as if they were strangers. Well, maybe they were. Their relationship had developed at a rapid pace, and Matt's health crisis had hit them so soon after they got together. Many things had never been said, and many questions were never asked or answered. He meant it. He wanted to start over.

Was she still angry? Hurt? He couldn't be sure after their brief conversation. She looked so good. Some of the weight she lost after the surgery had returned, and even in the baggy scrubs she wore, he could see her alluring curves. He loved seeing her hair caught up in the ponytail she always wore at work. He could remember her taking it down when she got home each night and seeing it cascade around her shoulders.

He had spent many lonely nights berating himself for mistreating Angela. Now that he was no longer in a state of shock and denial, he remembered Angela had told him about Dean and the baby she had given up for adoption. She had even told him she didn't want to do it, but she had a pulmonary embolism and lapsed into a coma. Why had he not remembered that when she tried explaining things to him?

He had been a fool, but maybe it wasn't too late.

~

GILL'S FINS and Fish Shack was located at the end of a pier on the beach. The charming wooden structure blended with the natural surroundings. The whitewashed walls adorned with nautical-themed decorations evoked a sense of maritime adventure, while large, open windows provided panoramic views of the sparkling Pacific Ocean and breathtaking sunsets.

They chose a table by the window, and although Jimmy would have preferred to sit beside her, she took the chair opposite his. At least he could get his fill of looking at her.

The waiter brought menus, water, and a small loaf of brown bread still steaming from the oven.

"The variety of seafood is incredible for such a small place," Jimmy explained. "You expect to find shrimp, sole, and snapper on the menu, but the specials include sand dabs, oysters, clam strips, and salmon. They will usually prepare the fish in four different ways. Regular, blackened, Cajun, garlic, and lemon pepper."

"You sound like the head waiter," she said as she reached for the bread.

"I was a waiter here when I was in college. The tips were great, and I could eat all the fish I wanted."

She looked surprised, so he continued. "You know, Angela. My parents are just hard-working people. I didn't have money until I got drafted into the majors."

"It's easy for me to forget that now. The house you live in would make anyone think you're living the high life. I don't mean that in a bad way. I know you worked hard for what you have."

"I did, but I was lucky, too. I have had some incredible breaks in life. I try to pay it forward if I can."

"What do you mean?"

"Well, I work with underprivileged kids and teach them the fundamentals of baseball. They might not make it to the majors, but hopefully, they will have friends and lots of fun."

"I think that's great. You never said."

"No reason to. This is just another example of how many things we don't know about one another."

The waiter appeared, and they both ordered grilled sand dabs and garden salads. Angela ran her hand across the crisp white tablecloth. And then put her fingers up to her neck to touch the angel necklace Dean had given her. Jimmy knew she did that to comfort herself in situations in which she felt uneasy. He wondered if he could ever comfort her as well as Dean had.

"It's your turn," he said.

She put down her fork and wiped her mouth with a napkin. "For what?" she said.

"To tell me something else about you."

She charmingly placed her index finger under her chin and looked upward. 'Hmm, let me think about it." She took a sip of water and said, "I love antiques. I've spent hours in antique shops searching for the perfect lamp. So far, no luck."

Jimmy thought about his house's ultrachic and modern

furnishings and wondered if she had felt uncomfortable there. He had often found it cold and without character, but he was away so often it didn't bother him, and he had grown used to it.

"We could drive up the coast one day. There are several quaint curio and antique shops that tourists frequent. I've never been, but it could be interesting," he said.

Jimmy swallowed another bite of the crisp green salad before continuing. "If you could design your own house just how you wanted to, what would it look like?"

She paused again but had a ready answer. She must have thought about this before. "I would build an updated replica of my grandmother's house. It was cozy and comfortable and always smelled like cinnamon and cloves. Of course, I would add modern bathrooms and an updated kitchen with new appliances. All the bedrooms would have big windows, but the walls would still be painted pale blue. Ideally, it would have a sea view. But that's a dream."

For the first time, she appeared relaxed, and he thought it might be because she was thinking of her grandmother, who was the person who had loved her best. He wanted to be that person for her, but first, he had to earn her trust again.

"That sounds nice," Jimmy said. "Would you like to go for a walk along the beach?"

"I would love that," she said.

So, they strolled in comfortable silence while listening to the rhythmic waves and the squawking seagulls. The sea air was refreshing, and Jimmy thought their date was a success, even if she had never reached for his hand.

CHAPTER 39

She and Jimmy had enjoyed several dates over the past few weeks, and he and Matt were both disappointed when she said she would have to work on Thanksgiving Day. She wasn't ready to map out her future yet, but she had changed her mind about leaving California. Finding her son was a miracle; she could not leave him again. Not ever. When she told Jimmy she was staying to be close to Matt, he said it was time that Matt knew she was his mother.

They agreed they would never expose Cindy's shady deal because it would hurt Matt too much to know. Jimmy told Angela he trusted her to explain things to Matt however she chose.

Today was the day. She was so nervous that her hands were shaking when she rang the doorbell. She heard Patches yelp, and moments later, Matt opened the door. Joy flooded his face. "Angela, it's you." He stepped into her open arms and gave her a long hug.

"Hi, big guy. You're looking better every time I see you."

"I'm so glad to see you. We missed you so much at Thanksgiving dinner. Everybody missed you."

"Well, I missed the whole family, too. I'll be there for Christmas this year, so we'll have a big celebration then."

"That's great news. I can't wait. I already bought Patches some treats."

"Dad's in his office. Do you want me to get him?"

"Not right now. It's you I came to see. I have a long story to tell you. Let's go outside so Patches can play."

They sat on the patio's edge, bare feet in the grass. Angela took Matt's hand and began explaining the complicated birth story.

"You know you're adopted, Matt, so you really have two moms and two dads. I want to tell you about your birth mother, who fell in love with your birth father and became pregnant with you. His name was Dean, and he died in an accident before you were born. She was only sixteen years old, and when she was in the hospital giving birth to you, she got very ill and almost died. She wasn't married, and she was too young to take good care of you, so a loving couple who really wanted a baby adopted you."

"You mean Dad and Mom?"

"Yes, Jimmy and Cindy adopted you, and they loved you from the moment they saw you."

"I guess I'm lucky."

"You certainly are. You have great parents, and your grandparents are special too."

"I meant I was lucky to have two sets of parents. Most kids don't. You said my dad died, right?"

"Yes, He was only seventeen years old."

"What happened to my mom?"

"Now the story gets interesting. Remember when you and your dad brought Patches into the clinic? I felt a connection with you, but I didn't know why. I loved you instantly." She gently ran her hand through his hair.

He looked up at her with Dean's eyes and smiled. "You did?"

"Yes, I did. Then, when you needed a liver transplant, I found out I was a match. While I was in the hospital, I had a dream about Dean, and I figured out what was going on. I had to be sure, so I asked you when your birthday was."

"March 20th."

"Yes, and when you told me that, I knew."

"Knew what?"

She turned to look at him with all the love she felt shining in her eyes. "That you are my son. You're the baby I gave birth to and the boy I've cried for at night and missed all these years. I am your birth mother, honey, and I love you so much."

He showed no surprise at her admission. "Is that why you donated a piece of your liver to save me?"

"No, I didn't know you were mine at the time. But giving you a piece of my liver was an easy decision. You've always had my heart."

∼

JIMMY TOOK ANGELA, Matt, and Patches to the beach the next day. While Matt and his dog waded in the surf, Jimmy and Angela placed a blanket on the sand and set out a picnic lunch.

"I've never seen him so excited," Jimmy said. "After you left, he came bouncing into my study to ask me how long I'd known and why I hadn't told him?"

"Did he understand I wanted to tell him myself?"

"Yes, and those were his only questions. I'm sure he will have more when he gets older, or maybe not. He's pretty happy about it. He called all four of his grandparents and blew their minds. I could hear him saying, "Can you believe it? I have two moms and two dads.

"I didn't think he would shun me, but I never expected such complete acceptance and understanding from a twelve-year-old boy," Angela said.

"That's because he is almost thirteen." They both grinned, knowing those words were straight from Matt's mouth.

"Thank you, Jimmy, for trusting me to handle this delicate matter." She leaned in and kissed him on the lips.

Instead of answering her, he cupped her neck, pulled her closer, and devoured her mouth. She responded with a guttural sound that excited him. "If we were alone, this food would be all over the sand, and I would be all over you."

"And I would welcome that, Jimmy. You've been patient and given me time and space to process all my complicated feelings. It wasn't all your fault. I know that now. The timing was all wrong, and I should have told you as soon as I suspected Matt was my son."

"So, are you saying you forgive me?"

"I am saying that. You hurt me very badly, but my heart has already begun to heal. I love and miss you both so much."

"Will you come back to Matt and me so we can be a family?"

"Yes, I want to do that soon."

Jimmy let out a whoop of delight, pulled her into his arms, and twirled her around. Matt heard the commotion, and he and Patches came running.

"We have to go now," Jimmy said to everyone's surprise.

"What?" Matt said. "Why? What about lunch?"

"We'll eat this at home. Hurry. Pack it all up, and let's go. It's time to show Angela our surprise."

Matt trembled with excitement. So soon? I thought you said—"

"Shh, don't spoil it. Hold that thought for just a while longer."

Matt made a zipper motion with his fingers.

~

THEY DROVE north toward Jimmy's house, but instead of turning left, they stayed on the beach highway and traveled a few miles further. Jimmy stopped in front of a small building with the words Surfside Realty painted on a large sign. Patches stayed in the car when they went inside. Matt was pulling on Angela's hand to hurry her along. A tall man greeted them with a voice as big as his belly.

"Well, there you are. I thought you said it might be a long time before you came back, but you would be back."

"I did say that Mr. Harper, but the time is now. If you would be so kind as to get out the photos and give us a few moments of privacy."

Matt squealed.

"What the heck is going on here?" Angela said.

"Can I show her, Dad? Can I?"

Jimmy grinned. "Go for it!"

Matt took her hand and led her to a table where two photos were displayed. One of them depicted a beautiful stretch of beach. In the second one, the camera pointed east toward the dunes above the beach. "What do you think, Angela? Do you like it?"

"It's beautiful. I love it. Are we going to picnic there?"

Matt giggled uncontrollably. "No, we're going to live there."

"What? Who is? What do you mean?"

"Dad's having a house built for you." He pointed up toward the dunes in the second photo. "He already bought the land. It's right up there."

She turned and locked eyes with Jimmy. "You're doing what, Jimmy Ross?"

"You described your dream house to me, so I hired an architect who will confer with you and build it exactly how you want, with blue bedroom walls and big ocean-facing windows."

Her eyes registered shock and disbelief, followed by the most beautiful look of acceptance and joy. She would never again worry about their compatibility or the differences in their backgrounds and financial circumstances. Jimmy truly loved her and Matt. She had found her precious son and her forever person. All her dreams had come true.

∽

THANK you for reading *Angel's Heart*. If you enjoyed this book you will love, *Accidental Angel*, the first book in the series. Some of the interesting characters including Hollywood Madden, Shane Madden and Dena Madden appear in both.

We invite you to subscribe to our newsletter and claim your FREE copy of *Until Forever Finds Us*, a heart-tugging romantic short story. You will find it here. https://BookHip.com/NDSGDQK

Thanks so much for reading our book. Please consider leaving us a review on our Amazon book page or on Goodreads. Reviews do not have to summarize the book, and they do not have to be long. We appreciate everyone who takes the time to help us by writing a few words. Reviews are so important and help us enter contests and win awards.

Amazon Review Page
https://amzn.to/47uqwIM

Goodreads Review Page
https://bit.ly/3YzvEat

ACKNOWLEDGMENTS

Our heartfelt thanks go out to our ARC team including Jerry Tess, Roger Thompson, Chaz, Carolyn Wilhelm, Susan Rowald, Lori Porter, Diane Colbert, Brenda Hill, and Alice Shepherd. We really appreciate the comments and the suggestions.

Charlene – I want to especially thank my amazing husband, Jerry, for doing so many things for me, so that I have time to write. Jerry is the first one to read my manuscripts and provides invaluable comments and corrections. He really is my treasure.

Judi – Thanks to Roger. He makes it so easy for me to write.

ABOUT THE AUTHORS

Charlene Tess and Judi Thompson are sisters who live in cities over 1400 miles apart. They combined their two last names into the pen name Tess Thompson and write novels as a team.

Judi Thompson has been writing since her early teens. She lives with her husband Roger in Texas. She is a retired supervisor for special education in a local school district.

Charlene Tess is a retired writing teacher and writes educational materials and grammar workbooks available on TPT.com. She lives with her husband Jerry in Colorado.

CONNECT WITH US ON SOCIAL MEDIA

Subscribe to our newsletter and claim a FREE eBook.
https://BookHip.com/NDSGDQK
Facebook: https://bit.ly/3GCGoek
Twitter: https://bit.ly/3FDoUx3
Amazon Book Page: https://amzn.to/3dfTfJR
Goodreads Book Page: https://bit.ly/3rpLrLD
Email us: NovelsbyTessThompson@gmail.com

Books by Charlene TESS and Judi THOMPSON
www.amazon.com/author/charlenetess
www.amazon.com/author/judithompson

- **Second Daughter (standalone novel)**
- **Secondhand Hearts series**
- **Dixieland Danger series**
- **Chance O' Brien series**
- **Angel Falls series**
- **Texas Plains romantic comedy series**

Scan the QR code below to claim your FREE copy of *Until Forever Finds U*s, a heart-tugging romantic short story.

https://BookHip.com/NDSGDQK

Made in the USA
Monee, IL
20 March 2025